A CHEQUE FOR THREE THOUSAND

BY

ARTHUR HENRY VEYSEY

NEW YORK

G. W. Dillingham Co., Publishers

MDCCCXCVII

Transcribed and edited by Jeffrey Merrow, November, 2014.

Published by Tadalique and Company, Cincinnati, Ohio.
Publisher web site: www.tadalique.com

Ordering Information:
For details, contact: webmaster@tadalique.com

ISBN: 978-1-952153-12-9

Printed in the United States of America.

CONTENTS.

A CHEQUE FOR THREE THOUSAND

CHAPTER I.

PLEASURES BY PROXY.

FOR the greater part of an hour, old Mr. Whitehurst, senior member of the banking firm of Whitehurst & Crandal, had been cutting off coupons in one of the subterranean vaults of the Mutual Safe Deposit Company. The close air made his head ache. As he turned the key on his stocks and bonds, he wondered if he was any happier than the youngest clerk in his bank, who just then was frowning over two long columns of figures that refused to tally. So that when the office boy handed him the card of the Reverend Wellesley Smith, he lost all patience.

"Tell him I'm not in," he cried, crustily. "Shall I never have any peace? He's after some more money. I know it. I could swear to it. More money! It's always money! Money, money, money. Bah! A pert miss with a charity ticket; a parson after a church window; a president after a new dormitory—they're all one, and I'm sick of 'em all. Every one of 'em. Still, I suppose I must see the man. You may tell Mr. Smith to step in."

"Yes, sir," said the office boy, who was not a little amazed at this unusual vehemence.

"I trust I see you well, Mr. Whitehurst, sir." The president of Calvin College shook the millionaire's hand with a gentle deference born of respect and fear. "And Mrs. and Miss Whitehurst, are they still abroad?"

"Yes; they are in Paris, spending money faster than I can make it," grumbled the old man. "But what d'ye want, Smith? I'm tired and my head aches, and I shall be obliged to you if you can come straight to the point. It's about Calvin College, eh?"

The Reverend Wellesley Smith hesitated, then began to skirmish cautiously.

"Calvin College is remarkably prosperous, sir, I am glad to say, thanks to your unstinted generosity."

"You do want money. I can tell by the way you begin. How much do you want this time and what's it for?"

"Ahem! just how much would depend upon—"

"I said how much."

"Three thousand would be more than I could expect after your—"

"And what's this three thousand to be for?"

"Miss Elizabeth Jones has promised fifty thousand to endow a professorship in biology if we can raise a like amount in six months."

Mr. Whitehurst took a cheque-book out of his drawer and promptly signed a cheque for the sum that the president had named.

"Here you are, Smith. But I tell you frankly, I am tired of this charity business[1], it's the humbug of my life. I might as well be one of those fellows who work the crank of a ticket-chopper on an elevated station for all the enjoyment that I get out of my life. I am simply a machine. A machine, sir, to turn out money. That's all."

"But, Mr. Whitehurst, sir," said the president of Calvin College, soothingly, "it is a noble inspiration to realize that you are simply the steward of the wealth with which Providence has graciously blessed you."

The old man shook his head doggedly.

"That may or may not be, Smith, but I do know this much. I have given thousands, I was going to say millions, to hospitals and churches and colleges, but—pshaw! bricks and mortar don't kindle a glow about your heart and make you feel that it is better to give than to receive. I have a keener enjoyment in giving one dime to a hurdy-gurdy man, or a penny stick of candy to a little beggar child, than I get out of a thousand dollars' worth of brick and mortar."

The college president fidgeted in his chair and picked up his hat to go. But he was not to escape so easily.

"For fifty years I have never wasted one cent. It seems as if I might have a holiday for once. Smith, I should like to go on a spree."

"Go on a spree?" repeated that gentleman, holding up his black-gloved hands.

"Yes; a spree."

"Do you mean, Mr. Whitehurst—but no, you cannot mean that you would imbibe freely, indulge unduly in alcoholic stimulants?"

Silas Whitehurst guffawed hoarsely.

"Say that I get a scapegoat, then. Send someone else on the spree?"

"Sir, you surprise me. That would be encouraging vice, sir."

"Come, come, Smith, you needn't look so shocked, man. I am not so black a sheep as you think me."

"I thought you could scarcely mean anything so dreadful," said the college president, very much relieved.

"But what I do mean is this: I am tired of this decorous doling out of cheques to you college presidents and ministers. You spend the money in a proper enough way, I grant that. But I want to do something improper for a change. I should like for once—for once, you are to understand, for a spree—to place a sum of money in the hands of a person who never asked me for it, who never dreamed of getting it, and see what he would do with it."

"In the hands of a person with whom you are not acquainted, Mr. Whitehurst, perhaps an utterly irresponsible person?"

"Exactly that," said the millionaire, stubbornly. "I remember when I was a young fellow earning ten dollars a week, many and many a night I have left the store too tired to think; and I used to amuse myself by wondering just what I should do if any one was fool enough to put a cheque for a thousand dollars in my hand at the very moment I was wishing for it and say: 'You would do such and such a thing if you had a thousand dollars, eh? Well, here is your thousand dollars. Now go and do it.' And there must be just such young chaps, dozens of 'em right here in New York, thinking the same thing at this very moment. Sometimes I think I should like to meet one of those young fellows—I should like to hunt one of them up. At times I feel like parading the streets as Providence, Smith."

The Reverend Wellesley Smith was speechless.

"Supposing I were to do it for once?"

The millionaire looked at the president wistfully. But the scholar could not possibly countenance such folly and glared sternly in his hat.

"Only once, Smith, for a spree."

The president of Calvin began to weaken. A certain amount of deference was due to so generous a patron. "It seems a most irrational way of doing—"

"Irrational? That, Smith, is exactly the word. I've worried over everything, I've thought over everything, I've weighed everything so conscientiously (all out of regard to you preachers) that I should like to do something irrational for a change. I want a spree, I tell you. I have a mind to take one. I should like to give a tolerably large sum of money to the first young fellow who took my fancy. And if the young fellow proved to be more irrational in spending the money than I was in the giving of it, why I should have all the bigger spree. After a specified time I would have him report to me how he had spent the money. That would be the only condition he would have to subscribe to. He should be the scapegoat to bear my follies. And I say that would be the next best thing to being young again yourself and spending it yourself."

The president looked at the millionaire fascinated. "To do so would assuredly be contrary to all recognized laws of economics and sociology, Mr. Whitehurst, and yet—"

"The laws of sociology and economics may go to the dickens for once. Because as surely as my name is Silas Whitehurst I'll do it. Smith, I tell you I am going to do it. Do you hear?"

A ghost of a smile played about Mr. Smith's thin lips. "And no doubt without great difficulty I might introduce to your notice a deserving young man of Calvin College, to whom a fellowship—"

"No, no, Smith. This goes to no deserving young prig of Calvin College." Silas Whitehurst was writing another cheque. "You get none of this money."

"How much is it, Mr. Whitehurst, sir?"

"It's a cheque for three thousand," cried the millionaire, waving it excitedly in the air. "And it's for the first young man whose face I choose to take a fancy to and who looks to me as if he could make me laugh for an hour or two by telling me how he had spent it. I don't care how he spends it. The crazier the better. All I shall ask of him is, that he be honest and clean."

"That is a large sum of money to give away in so inconsequential a manner," remonstrated the president seriously.

"I don't care. I am going to have my fling for once. And don't you go spoiling my fun by preaching, Smith. Because I won't listen. I may be an old fool. I have a vague idea that I am. But I'll do it. I'll play the fool for once. I'll take my pleasure by proxy. And while my conscience is taking a rest, I'll be making hay. While the sun is shining on this very day of February the third, eighteen hundred and ninety-five. I am going to find my scapegoat. At once, I tell you. Now, Smith, you had better come along and see the fun. Because it will be worth your while, I warrant you."

"I thank you," the president of Calvin answered dryly, "but I must spare no endeavor to secure the twenty-four thousand dollars yet needed to make the munificent gift of Miss Elizabeth Jones ours beyond peradventure. I wish you a good-morning, Mr. Whitehurst, sir, and I thank you for your generous aid."

"Good-bye, Smith." Silas Whitehurst struggled into his overcoat grumbling. "That man has nothing human in him. I venture to say that the fellow who gets this won't be so lukewarm."

He put the cheque carefully in his pocketbook, and sallied down Broadway to find a young man with original ideas and a clever but honest face who might happen to have use for three thousand dollars.

CHAPTER II.

WANTED: A SCAPEGOAT.

From nine o'clock in the morning till half past one, Mr. Whitehurst, senior member of the banking-house of Whitehurst & Crandal, tramped the streets, eagerly searching for a young man who should answer to his somewhat novel requirements.

His mysterious air caused more than one policeman to entertain grave suspicions. If two pleasant fellows, talking animatedly side by side, happened to engage the millionaire's attention, he squeezed up beside them, or dogged their footsteps with unflagging zeal, while he listened anxiously to their talk. He haunted the hotel corridors. He journeyed to and fro on the ferry-boats. He rode on the elevated trains beside likely young men from Battery Place to Harlem.

But the world seemed all at once to get along very well without millionaires. Apparently no young man was on the lookout for a genial impersonator of Providence who should benignly wave a three thousand dollar cheque in his face. Mr. Whitehurst began to be a little ashamed of the dreams of his youth. The young men of to-day were more practical, it appeared. Hunting young fellows with extravagant ideas and attractive faces was more tiresome than he had thought that it would be. It is true that more than once he had occasion to prick up his ears in the lobbies of hotels. But only to be repeatedly disappointed. Nothing should induce him to spend the cheque in helping anyone out of a business difficulty. Mr. Whitehurst scorned anything so prosaic. The interest must be there or he would carry the cheque back to the bank. He insisted upon a little excitement, a little romance. More than once a bright face arrested his attention. And the boot-black that polished his shoes actually confessed to him that if he had a few hundred dollars, he would buy a broncho and revolvers and immediately go out West to hunt buffaloes and Indians like the hero that he had just been reading about. That interested Mr. Whitehurst very much indeed, only he was afraid that the scheme was too big for the small boot-black.

So that about lunch time, Mr. Whitehurst turned into Bleecker Street very much discouraged. He wished that the boot-black had been a few years older. He wondered if he did not possess possibilities. And while he was wondering, a savory odor of broiled beefsteak came floating out of a restaurant; and he realized that he was hungry. He looked in to see if the place might be clean. He saw a great many strange-looking people eating at little round tables. "If any of those artist fellows haven't any use for my cheque, I might as well go home," he thought. He entered deliberately and walked very slowly up the long room, scanning each face closely as he passed.

Then suddenly out of the din of shuffling feet, clattering of dishes and the hubbub of conversation, these words sounded clearly.

"A thousand dollars, Richardson, only a thousand, or while I am wishing at all, why shouldn't I wish for three thousand?"

In his excitement, Mr. Whitehurst jostled a waiter and nearly upset his dishes. He knew at once that he had found his man. There he was—a tall, straight-limbed young fellow of twenty-five. His face was as frank and fresh as a schoolboy's. "And just such a laugh as I had when I was a youngster," muttered the millionaire, as he seated himself at the next table.

This young gentleman, however, quite unconscious of the kind old eyes that rested on him, or of the three thousand dollar cheque that was actually hovering over him like a beneficent angel, leaned back in his seat, stretched out his long legs, thrust his hands in his trousers pockets, and sighed profoundly.

"A thousand dollars! Why that would make me free—a man, famous, perhaps."

"But you haven't it, my dear fellow; and what is the good of dreaming about it and torturing yourself in that way. It's childish," remonstrated the other.

Silas Whitehurst spilled his soup in his excitement. "That is all you know," he chuckled, nodding his head toward the one addressed as Richardson.

"Of course. But why shouldn't I suppose for the lark that I did have it?"

"Certainly; if that sort of thing amuses you.

"It does amuse me immensely. Because supposing is the next best thing to having, isn't it?"

His friend laughed good-naturedly. "Suppose away, then. Well, what would you do with the money, if you had it?" he asked carelessly, looking at some girls who had just entered the restaurant.

"What would I do? I'll tell you precisely what I should do. First of all I should go to that son of Hanan, the city-editor, and say: 'For two years I have been ruining my nerves and stomach, and living less comfortably than a hod-carrier, in scouring the unclean places of this city, in writing lurid biographies of thieves and murderers and other undesirable people.

But now I am going to live.'"

The cynical young man laughed and flicked the ashes off his cigar. "And what then?"

"Why then, having shaken the dust of the newspaper office off my shoes forever, I should begin to write the Great Play."

The cynical young man was flirting with the girls who had attracted his attention, and was an indifferent listener. But Silas Whitehurst knew that he had found his man, and listened, fascinated.

"Not that I have any fault to find with the newspaper life. I have just what I wanted. I have experience. I know what life is. But now when it's time for me to have done with the business, if I would accomplish things, I am bound hand and foot."

"Yes?" queried his friend, absent-mindedly.

"But with three thousand dollars in my pocket, nothing could be easier than my life for the next year or two. With moderate economy I could live very well indeed on a thousand a year in a vine-covered villa near Naples, say, or in a cottage off the coast of Brittany."

"You are a romantic beggar, altogether too much so for a reporter who is living on eighteen dollars a week. I want to see some people I know over there. I shall be back in a minute."

The first impulse of Silas Whitehurst was to make himself known to the would-be dramatist; but on second thoughts, he preferred to pose as a mysterious benefactor. That was more in keeping with the ridiculous rôle that he had assumed for the day with so much enjoyment. And if the story of his strange experiment in philanthropy should leak out, as no doubt it would, there would be endless begging letters. He had no intention of being a good angel to every young man that cherished romantic ideas. That would be embarrassing, decidedly. So he tore a leaf out of his commonplace book, and wrote these words in a cramped, jerky hand:

"Young Man: I never set eyes on you till to-day. But I like the looks of your face, and I happened to overhear what you have been saying to your friend. I don't know the A B C's of play-writing, and I am quite sure that reporters are the pest of my life; but if you want to leave newspaper life and scribble plays, I am going to give you a fair chance. A cheque for three thousand dollars ($3,000) will be waiting for you in the office of Howe & Williamson, my attorneys, and signed by Mr. George H. Howe, made payable to bearer, in half an hour, if you take the trouble to send for it; and if you tear off the agreement written below, simply to show that you are willing to do what I ask of you. It's not your affair to question why I happen to give you the money. All you have to do is to send the agreement named to the office of Howe & Williamson, Guarantee Loan Building, by a messenger before nine o'clock to-night. That, sir, is your business. I shall see that the cheque is sent back. Why I choose to believe in you is my affair, I hope. You are to understand clearly that my attorney, Mr. Howe, will sign the cheque if you have the faith to send for it, (which I doubt), so there is no use in trying to thank me or to try to find out who I am."

The agreement was as follows:

February 3, 1895.

"For value received, I promise to report in person, one year from date, at the office of Howe & Williamson, how I shall have spent the three thousand dollars."

This extraordinary document written and folded, Mr. Whitehurst called a waiter.

"Waiter," he whispered mysteriously, "you see that young fellow at my right. Well, give this note to him as soon as I leave this room. Do you understand, now?"

"Sutin', suh," answered the waiter.

After giving these instructions, Mr. Silas Whitehurst looked long and affectionately at his protégé; then, well pleased with his morning's work, he walked to Broadway, and boarded a car that carried him to the office of his attorneys.

CHAPTER III.

A TIDE THAT LEADS TO FORTUNE.

Norman Bridgworth Pennington had seen strange things happen during his two years' connection with the New York *Courier.* He had interviewed servants who had inherited titles. He had seen fortunes spring up like mushrooms in a single night. But it is one thing to see strange things happen to other people, and quite another to have them happen to yourself.

Three times he read the cramped handwriting of the note that the waiter had given him. Then he looked around the room cautiously and sheepishly. Some practical joker, perhaps, overhearing the somewhat foolish conversation that he had had with his friend Richardson, had taken liberties. It was, however, very difficult for him to guess who seemed likely to have done it. He summoned the waiter.

"Waiter," he cried angrily, "who gave you this note?"

The waiter shook his woolly head. "Befo' de Lawd, suh, I dunno. Ole gent, suh. White hyar, suh."

"Didn't he look peculiar to you in any way?"

"Heh? Peculiar? I dunno. No, suh, jest oranary gent, suh."

"What did he say to you when he gave you the note?"

"He jest gib me dis hyar note, suh, an' he say, 'you is to gib dis hyar note to dat young fellah,' 'xcuse lib'ty, suh, but dem's de 'dentical wuds, suh, 'to dat young fellah as soon as I leave dis room.' An' he gib me a dollar to do it, suh," added the waiter suggestively.

Pennington looked around for his friend who was standing at the desk about to pay his bill. He beckoned him back. "What do you want now, Pen?" he cried impatiently. "You know we are late, I suppose."

"I won't keep you more than a minute," answered Pennington, nervously pulling at his mustache. "But did you happen to notice the old gentleman that sat at the table next to us?"

Richardson stared. "My dear boy, we have no time now to concern ourselves with old gentlemen that happen to sit next to us at the table. We are due at the office of the *Courier*."

"But I am in earnest; I have a good reason for asking. Did he strike you as being quite—well, quite rational?"

"Is it good for a story?" asked Richardson, with a sudden interest.

"I think it is. Perhaps one of the best."

Richardson sat down at the table and tipped his hat on the back of his head. If there is one thing a good reporter can do, he observe, and Richardson was one of the best reporters in the city.

"Old gentleman? Let me see. Yes; about seventy or seventy-five. Silk hat and gaiters—brown gaiters. Mutton-chop whiskers. Queer old face—lines a trifle stern. Eyes shrewd but kind. A businessman. Say a broker or a banker, and you can't be far from the mark. Successful, too. Has his eccentricities, no doubt. But rational? Yes; everything would point to his being rational, I should say. And while I think of it, he was drinking in all that precious moonshine of yours with more relish than I do a good case at the police-court. But sane enough, I should say."

Richardson paused inquiringly, while Pennington straightened out the note that he had crumpled up in his momentary anger.

"What do you think of that?" he asked.

Richardson handed it back laughing. "A subject for Ward's Island. Crazy; no doubt of it."

"I rather thought so myself." Pennington said the words with indifference, but he put the note in his pocket.

Presently, just before they entered the *Courier* Building, Richardson grasped his friend's arm. "You will laugh at me perhaps: but if you didn't fling away that note, I wish you would let me see it again."

He read it carefully, Pennington watched his face with a strange eagerness.

"Supposing that it were true, though," said Richardson, handing it back. "Queer things have happened before now, and you and I have seen some of them happen. Perhaps this time they are going to happen to you. I believe I should trace the matter up. There ought to be a story behind it at any rate. But if it should be true?" He whistled significantly.

Pennington gave a sigh of relief. "Do you know, I am awfully glad to hear you talk like that, Richardson. I may be foolish, but I shan't deny that I am impressed. I shall trace it up."

"And I would lose no time about it," said Richardson, entering the office of the *Courier*.

Pennington hesitated a moment, scanning the unusual communication once more. Then going to the District Messenger Office nearest the *Courier* Building, he tore off the agreement, signed it as directed, and gave it to a messenger-boy.

"Take this to the law-office of Howe & Williamson, boy, and be sure that you wait for an answer."

The boy ran out of the office, and Pennington went slowly upstairs to get his evening's assignments.

The city-editor snarled as he saw him. "Late again, Pennington, eh? Now I give you fair warning, sir. This is the last time, positively. You are always late. Do you flatter yourself that this office can't manage to exist without the aid of your valuable services? Because if you do, I shall feel it to be my painful duty to deprive you of that childish illusion."

Pennington had heard just such amiable pleasantries grace the lips of the city-editor many times before. The abuse had been endured as a matter of course. But to-night he was irritated beyond measure. "I thought I was on the track of a story, sir," he cried.

"Story," growled the city-editor, "what is it?"

Pennington related his late experience, the editor frowning impatiently. His comment was brief. "Pooh, sir, you are a fool. How many times have I told you to use your judgment? You gave credence to that story—a palpable fake? You wasted your time in—"

The door swung open and the messenger-boy put his head in: "Mr. Norman Pennington here?"

Pennington snatched the yellow envelope. He could scarcely tear it open, his hands trembled so violently. Not a line of explanation. But an oblong piece of paper—crisp, light-bluish, of unmistakable significance the world over. A cheque. Payable to order of bearer. And for three thousand dollars.

His dreams were no longer dreams. They had crystallized into facts. Everything he had ever dreamed to hope for had come true. Actually! In a moment!

CHAPTER IV.

WHEN DREAMS COME TRUE.

THE next morning Pennington was up with the sun. While he was dressing, Richardson came into his room, grumbling lazily at the noise that Pennington was making at such a weirdly early hour.

"I suppose you won't work to-day," said Richardson, watching his friend lay out his good clothes. "What are you going to do with yourself?"

"First of all I am going to take a cab and drive to Bowling Green. I shall buy a passage on the *New York*—she sails to-morrow at the foot of Fulton Street, 10 a.m. After that I shall get a decent breakfast. I have always wanted to breakfast well, but I have never had the chance before. Naturally I shall then make a few purchases."

Richardson began to whistle and then laughed. "You are rather in a hurry, aren't you?"

"Not at all. Didn't I tell you that I should do precisely that only yesterday?"

Richardson looked at his friend critically. "Do you think you are going to find it very much easier to write your Great Play in London or Paris than you would here in prosaic old New York?"

"I don't know what you mean," said Pennington uneasily.

"I mean that three thousand dollars is no fortune and that you are likely to do everything over there but write the Great Play."

"Oh!"

"There's danger of that, you know. I don't want to talk cant; but I do want to spare you the humiliation of sneaking back here to New York in a few months with the pleasantest of memories but with no Great Play."

"I say, but you are a good fellow," cried Pennington, seizing his friend's hand.

"I believe you, my boy. Well, I must be getting back to bed, and you had better be making your preparations. Going to Europe isn't exactly like taking a trip to Hoboken."

"The rush in getting off is half the fun."

Richardson went back to bed to finish his sleep and Pennington walked around the corner and jumped into a hansom. He was driven to the banking-house on which his cheque was drawn. Not without a tremor of anxiety did he present it, but it was accepted unhesitatingly.

"Just how will you have it, Mr. Pennington?" asked the teller who knew Pennington as a newspaper man.

"A letter of credit for twenty-two hundred, if you please, the rest in fifty dollar bills."

His pockets stuffed with money, he went to the offices of the American Line, where he engaged a passage on the *New York*. It was the winter season, of course, and he secured a comfortable stateroom on the spar-deck. The price of the stateroom was a little more than he had thought of paying, but the luxury of fresh air is worth a few extra dollars. Then he went to a tailor just off the Avenue, from whom he ordered two suits of clothes to be ready in twenty-four hours. The rest of his clothes he could get abroad.

"Now I can go to breakfast," he said. His breakfast at the Holland House was a rather elaborate affair for one who was to live two years on three thousand dollars. "But I must allow for first impulses, I suppose," he thought.

After he had spent half an hour over a fifty cent cigar (because to spoil a good meal by ending up with a bad cigar is absurd), he drove about from one place to another making purchases. He no longer despised the shoppers of West Twenty-third Street. So far in life it had called for Herculean efforts to keep two pair of trousers from bagging at the knees, and to avoid treading down the heels of one pair of shoes. And if any young man would know just what pleasure there is in buying at one time half a dozen suits of silk underwear or five pairs of shoes or twelve styles of neckwear—let him try to look decent and pay all his expenses (not to speak of his pleasures) on eighteen dollars a week.

One of the largest of his expenditures was not for himself. It was a snug little deposit in the Second National Bank for three hundred dollars in the name of Harriman Richardson, his friend, who, in a few weeks, hoped simultaneously to assume the responsibilities of a sub-editorship and marriage to a young woman as poor as himself.

But all this cost something. Just how much, Pennington deliberately compelled himself to be ignorant—for a few hours at least. He had no intention of spoiling his pleasure in buying things by inquiring the price of them. Had he kept an account, however, he would have been horrified to find nothing left out of the eight hundred dollars that he had put into his pocket that morning. As a matter of fact, when he had paid his bills the next morning, he had precisely twenty-one dollars left in ready cash.

And the account stood thus;

Cab fares	$7.00
Breakfast, lunch, and dinner for two	21.25
Steamship-ticket	100.00
Two suits of clothes	120.00
Shoes	20.00
One doz. shirts	20.00
Underwear, half doz	30.00
Hats, caps, etc.	50.00
Neckwear, gloves, collars, cuffs, handkerchiefs	17.75
Trunks, dress-suit cases, etc.	40.00
Rugs, steamer-chair	15.00
Overcoat	60.00
Deposit for Harriman Richardson.	300.00
Total	**$801.00**

CHAPTER V.

WHAT'S IN A NAME?

THERE is something about the sailing of an ocean greyhound that arouses the dullest imagination. No matter how familiarly one may walk up the gangway, and no matter how blasé one pretends to be, no one but a pork-butcher or a census-taker is really indifferent. Pennington neither felt blasé nor did he pretend to be. He toiled up the gangway with a dress-suit case in one hand and a huge bundle of canes and umbrellas in the other so eagerly that any one could see that he had never been abroad before. The scene itself was familiar enough. Often and often he had been the first to interview a statesman or an actress on their return from abroad. But then he was only the spectator. Now he was a part of the show itself. That makes all the difference in the world. And he felt as if things were very much changed about indeed, when, at the last moment, one of the reporters of the *Courier* came up to him breathless, and asked in all seriousness what were his plans in going abroad so soon.

Pennington was vastly amused. "Why, what's that to you, Jones?" he cried.

Jones made a comprehensive motion with his hands. "Nothing to me, my dear fellow, but to the world, everything."

"So I am a public character, am I?"

"Certainly. Haven't you seen the papers?"

Pennington took the copy of the *Courier* that the reporter held out to him and looked at it curiously. There was a long account of his strange good fortune and surmises as to who the author of it could be. A bad portrait of himself graced the front page. He glanced the account over, but when he came to the statement that he was to sail on the S. S. *New York* that morning, he first of all frowned, then he laughed heartily.

"My dear fellow," he whispered, "can you keep a secret? This is for your ears alone, understand, and not for the newspapers. I had no liking, you may be sure, of posing on board this boat as the beneficiary of eccentric millionaires, and I was rather certain that the *Courier* would make something of the story. So you will find no name on the list of cabin passengers as Norman B. Pennington. Henceforth know me as Norman B. Diggle of Montana."

Jones gasped. Richardson chuckled. "You might have chosen a more aristocratic name," he cried. "Halloa, there goes the whistle."

The friends clasped hands.

"Dear old Pen, good-bye. We have stuck pretty well together in life. Just what awaits you over there, I don't know. But when you get ready for it, there is a berth for you on the *Courier*."

"I hope I have done with the *Courier* forever," cried Pennington with fervor.

"And if you should get hard up, you will let me know?"

Pennington laughed. "With two thousand dollars in my pocket? They are getting ready to pull off the gangway. Think of me the day you marry Mary. I shall think of you. And, Jones, don't forget that what I have told you is not for the newspaper."

The ship's moorings were cast off. Slowly the *S. S. New York* moved away from her pier and Norman Bridgworth Pennington sailed away to strange lands to meet stranger adventures.

CHAPTER VI.

IT NEVER RAINS BUT IT POURS.

Before Pennington had been on board the *New York* twenty-four hours, he had ingratiated himself in the good-will of every passenger with whom he came into contact, and he took pains to come into contact with many. Even the aristocratic mammas of Washington Square and of Beacon Street, who, horrified at the vulgar appellation of Diggle, carefully spread the maternal wing to shield their daughters from his contaminating touch, were gradually disarmed by the gaiety[2] of his manner and the charm of his smile. Before the boat had passed Fire Island, the men had left the Mr. off the Diggle when addressing him. With the vulgar, the unattractive, and other people commonly supposed to be impossible, he was adored. The school-mistress from Concord talked Emerson with him; the candy-maker from Astoria, cruelly shunned because Nature had sardonically presented him with a cast in one eye, fixed the good eye on him with unflagging devotion and wide-awake energy. Even the young man going to London to seek work (could a more hopeless character be imagined?) looked less mournful when he heard Pennington laugh.

But it was with the widow, Sally Harris, that his conquest was absolute.

To such of the passengers as prided themselves on doing all things with due regard to the dictates of the fashionable world, Mrs. Sally Harris was sufficiently formidable. But Pennington cared very little for the dictates of the fashionable world. He wanted characters for his Great Play.

And from the moment that his eyes had taken in the green silk dress, the cork-screw curls, the wrinkled, fat and red old face, he hailed her as one of the low comedy characters. And Mrs. Harris returned the regard of Pennington with effusion. Hers was no lukewarm spirit.

"You see, Mr. Diggle, my dear (you don't mind a old woman callin' you, my dear, do you?) I feel that you are one of us. Diggle and Harris—the names sort of chime together."

"I'm glad you like my name, Mrs. Harris," said Pennington, demurely.

"Oh, but, lor, Diggle, that ain't the only reason that my old heart goes out to you. Nor just because you are good and kind. But because you are the very image of my dead Bob. So you be. He had a mustache like you; he was your 'eight; and he had a complexion like yours."

"That is very remarkable."

Pennington did not feel flattered.

"And he talked like you, dearie. He went to Hoxford, and he could hold his 'ead as high as any of 'em. But he died a year ago come Michelmas, and the best son that mother ever had."

When the theme of the dead Bob languished, so to speak, Mrs. Harris inquired into Pennington's past life with a tender solicitude. And he amused himself by relating to her melodramatic adventures of a fictitious career in Montana. Nothing was too extravagant for her belief.

"You a senator! For all that you are so young! Senator Diggle! It's wonderful! And you have roamed the wide prairies, and been a shepherd boy, and dug in silver mines with your hands. And now you're a millionaire and a M. P." The widow held up her hands and gazed admiringly.

"Though I've heard of just as wonderful happening in the States before, my dear. Silas Whitehurst, my dead husband's cousin (though you might 'a' thought he was my own brother, he was that kind), he left England fifty odd year ago without a pound in his pocket, and now he rides in his carriage and pair. But his daughter Dorothy is a stuck-up little minx."

"That is very remarkable, Mrs. Harris, but you won't tell anyone of all I've been telling you, will you?"

"Not a word, dearie, though you are too modest, and that's the truth of it."

But when Pennington amused himself by telling Mrs. Harris these idle tales of a phantom past, he did not dream that his imaginary adventures as cowboy, miner, millionaire and senator would go to other ears. He had not counted on the gossiping proclivities of the admiring widow.

He was horrified one day, then, to see her pointing at him; and he could not help overhearing the random words:

"Once a shepherd boy, my dear, then a-diggin' for gold and silver; and now worth his millions and ridin' in his own brooch, as 'aughty as Queen Victoria; and a orater in Parliament."

Pennington felt that his position had become unexpectedly embarrassing. And he dared not contradict those stories of Mrs. Harris.

He began to wonder if there might not be difficulty in assuming his own name once more, if, as was more than likely, any of the passengers of the *New York* should happen to run across him in London or Paris. Decidedly, the situation was awkward.

However, there was nothing for it now but to act the rôle of the ex-cowboy, millionaire and senator with vigor and spirit. So that when it was whispered about that the nice man with the horrid name was so great a personage, and when Mr. Stanley Powers, a stock-broker from Chicago, slapped him on the back and said that he was too modest by half, and that he owed it to the great and glorious West to show the effete East that they were some pumpkins out there, Pennington merely shook his head and said: "It is queer how people exaggerate things."

In consequence, the story of Mrs. Harris gained general credence among the passengers, and everybody agreed that it was beautiful to see a young man so modest.

Pennington was dozing. Mrs. Harris was reading the *Courier* that Jones had given Pennington the morning they sailed. There was a vivid ejaculation from Mrs. Harris: "For the land's sake!"

He opened one eye, lazily. Evidently the widow was not referring to any land actually in sight. Her face was purple with suppressed excitement.

"If here ain't the livin' breathin' picture of my dead Bob himself, that has walked into the front page of this newspaper, my name ain't Sally Harris, that's all." Pennington looked to where her fat forefinger was pointing, and saw the likeness of himself.

Meanwhile Mrs. Harris was reading the story of the three thousand dollar cheque with avidity. She laid the paper on her knees and rolled her eyes in ecstasy[3].

"It's heavenly. It reads like a bit out of a story-book. And the paper says that he was to go to England right on this ship. Norman Bridgworth Pennington! What a fine soundin' name? Do you know any such a person aboard, Diggle!"

"There is no one on the list of cabin passengers known by that name, I believe, Mrs. Harris," answered Pennington, smiling.

"What a heavenly way of givin' away money. Hundreds of pound have I gave away in my life-time, but I never got any good out of it. It seems to me that I would never like to see anything so intrestin' as that young man."

Pennington leaned over in his chair. "Mrs. Harris, can you keep a secret?"

She drew herself up with dignity. "I should 'ope I was hold enough to, Diggle."

Pennington hesitated. "She has spread the report broadcast of my being a millionaire[4] and senator. Just as surely will she tell my real name if I tell it to her. But can I find a better way of escaping from the name of Diggle and its associations?"

"Well, Diggle, I'm waitin'," said the widow, soberly.

"It would be well not to say too much about it, Mrs. Harris—but that three thousand dollars was given to me."

Mrs. Harris jumped up from her chair and then sat down slowly again, looking greatly concerned. "Diggle, my dear, are you off your head?"

"No; it is quite true. It is precisely as I say. That cheque was given to me. I am Norman B. Pennington.

She looked at him, bewildered.

Pennington told her the whole story.

"Then, do you mean to say that all that about you bein' a discoverer of silver mines is fictious?"

"It was only for a joke, you know."

"And you ain't a millionaire?" she asked, anxiously.

"I have just about two thousand dollars in the world."

"Then you ain't a millionaire. You ain't a penny to your name to speak of, and here you have been spendin' money like a young lord. Oh, you blessed fibber, I shall die laughin', yes, I shall, and no mistake."

"Mrs. Harris, Mrs. Harris, calm yourself," said Pennington, sternly. Mrs. Harris was poking him violently in the ribs, and doing other unseemly things. "I can see nothing so very funny in the situation."

"Funny! nothin' funny! And ain't you as poor as Job? Tell me that. And ain't you been as kind to me as if you were my own son Bob? Tell me that. And ain't you as near like my son Bob as if he were walkin' these decks this blessed minute? tell me that too. And then you see nothin' funny!" Here she was rendered speechless by a violent fit of coughing and laughter.

"I have heard much of the British sense of humor," said Pennington plaintively to himself, as he patted the old lady on the back, "but really, this quite exceeds my expectations."

Indeed, during the whole of the next day, the last of the voyage, Mrs. Harris' conduct awakened Pennington's apprehensions for her sanity. If, at the table, he happened to catch her eye, she promptly exploded into vulgar laughter. If she saw him appear on the deck, the symptoms of a fresh outburst assumed alarming proportions, so that it was necessary for him to turn his back on her and to gaze steadily out to sea. Nor was it an easy matter to ignore her or to snub her. Her gaze followed him about with a persistency only equalled by that of the one-eyed candy-maker of Astoria. But to his intense disappointment, he could hear nothing that gave him any reason to suppose that she had mentioned his real name to a single soul on board.

The next morning, the passengers awoke to find themselves at the pier in Southampton.

Pennington determined at the last moment that he would go to Paris immediately, because the majority of the passengers were going to London. And he thought that if he took the roundabout route of Folkstone to Boulogne and thus avoided the ordinary channel route of the Paris bound passengers of the American Line, he might escape the rest of them and drop the name of Diggle and his pseudo-past.

Mrs. Harris' farewell to him was no less affectionate than absurd. She laughed and cried by turns.

"I hope we may have the pleasure of seeing each other again in the near future," said Pennington, rather coldly.

"And which is it to be, my dear, Diggle or Pennington?"

"Pennington, let us trust, Mrs. Harris," said he with emphasis.

"Take an old woman's advice and stick to the Diggle. It's more nat'ral-like and savors more of Harris. I want to know if you would do me a tremenjous favor. Would you, dearie?"

"I am entirely at your service, Mrs. Harris," said Pennington pleasantly.

"Why I am only an old woman and you won't take it amiss if I leave you a little soov-neer?"

"Well really, you know, Mrs. Harris," protested Pennington vaguely.

"Come, now, Diggle, you ain't going to disappoint me are you, my dear?" she coaxed, looking at him very anxiously.

"But my name isn't[5] really Diggle, you know."

"Well, well, so you will take it, won't you? It's just a little odd trinket so that you will remember a silly old woman who has lost her own son and what loves you." She slipped something in Pennington's pocket. "But there's my train hootin' and whistlin' fit to drive you daft. Good-bye, me dear, and think sometimes of poor old Mrs. Harris."

"A most extraordinary woman," thought Pennington, watching the train leave the station. "I wonder what she can have put in my pocket?"

He drew out an envelope. "N. B. Diggle, Esq.," stretched across it, the N. beginning at the extreme left hand corner and the Esq. ending where it is customary to place the stamp. He broke the seal and took out two papers.

One of them read thus:

"I want my dear friend Diggle (though he does call himself Pennington, but I like Diggle better because it is more 'akin to Harris, so I *shall* call him it) to spend the amount of this little cheque as a remembrance of his affectionate friend, Sally Harris. And all I ask of him is that he must call on me one year come Christmas at twenty-eight Grosvenor Square, London, to tell me how he spends the money unless I shall be visiting my dead husband's cousin, Silas Whitehurst, at that time, when he need't come."

The other was more orthodox in character. It was a cheque on Brown, Shipley & Co., and it read thus—

"Pay to N. B. Diggle two thousand pounds.

Sally Harris."

CHAPTER VII.

ALL THE WORLD LOVES A HERO.

WHEN Pennington assumed the pseudonym of N. B. Diggle of Montana, that he might escape the notoriety that would otherwise doubtless have been his on board the *S. S. New York*, he had, of course, not the remotest idea that such a person as N. B. Diggle of Montana actually existed in the flesh. But such was the case.

And strangely enough, the previous history of the real Mr. Diggle of Butte, Montana, corresponded in the main to the fictitious history conjured up in the fertile brain of the false Mr. Diggle. In his early days, the true Diggle had led a wild and somewhat precarious existence as a cowboy; he had really discovered a silver mine while digging the foundations of his cellar; and, lastly, he had done his country service by serving a term in the State Senate.

Here, however, comes the real ground for wonder and surprise (though the thoughtful reader will have observed that Nature, when devising her little jokes, does not do things by halves). On the identical day that Pennington confessed to Mrs. Harris that his name was not really Diggle, the real Senator Napoleon Bonaparte Diggle of Butte, Montana, was actually seated at one of the little round tables of the Boulevard de la Madeleine.

Senator Napoleon B. Diggle was ill at ease. Senator Diggle was unhappy. He was lonely. He listened with a pained melancholy to what he harshly termed "the cussed gibberish of froggies." His breakfast had consisted of three rolls and a cup of coffee, and he was hungry. He had no use whatever for a country that did not know the delicacy of corned beef and cabbage, not to speak of a good cigar. He sneered at the baggy trousers of the French soldiers. The whiskers of the men excited his unbounded derision; the dresses of the women, his contempt. It is true, he had expected all this. Before he left Butte, he knew perfectly well that only one country all the world could boast of absolutely noble-institutions, of a perfect government, and of beautiful women and manly men. He had not come all the way from Butte to be sure of this. The whole French race—people and history—he had always considered as beneath contempt. With one glorious exception, his namesake, Napoleon.

Senator Diggle's passion for things Napoleonic was hereditary. He bore his Christian name with great pride. When as a cowboy, many years before, he had ridden around the cattle in the stillness of night, his father had often fought over with him the battles of Napoleon. Abbott's life of Napoleon Bonaparte was young Napoleon Diggle's Shakespeare. And with the advance of years, this passion for things Napoleonic had become[6] a mania. He lamented his height of six feet three inches because Napoleon was short. He was rude in his manners, because Napoleon had been rude. He was clean-shaven and protruded his lower jaw, because to be clean-shaven and to protrude the lower jaw he considered to be Napoleonic. In the Senate of his State he was familiarly addressed as Nap. Diggle, because, when he engaged in debate, and that was often, he assumed the attitude commonly supposed to be characteristic of his hero. To deferentially allude to him as the Napoleon of finance, was just as good as getting your hand in his pocket.

Such was Senator Napoleon Bonaparte Diggle of the flesh, and he had come abroad for two cherished purposes. One of these, and the foremost, was to pay his tribute to the spirit of the great general at the tomb of Napoleon. The other was to hunt lions in Africa.

The latter purpose, however, was not for a moment to be placed side by side with anything Napoleonic. To see the tomb of Napoleon—that was his Mecca. When he had done that reverence, he wished to try his hand at lion-killing, but that was merely an after-thought, a trivial recreation. And although he had arrived in Paris only that morning, it was his intention to leave for Marseilles *en route* for Africa before night. He prided himself on doing things quickly. "It is Napoleonic," he said.

The coffee drunk, the rolls nibbled, Senator Diggle walked slowly towards the Boulevard des Italiens to get a cab. A step or two from the café, brought him to one of those establishments so common to France, where one may buy artificial wreaths and other suitable funereal adornments. A flash of joy illuminated Senator Diggle's face. He would buy one of those wreaths and lay it on the tomb of Napoleon as a tribute of respect from America to France, from Senator Napoleon Diggle to General Napoleon Bonaparte.

He entered the shop and pointed to an immense wreath. "I want the very best of the caboodle," he cried with enthusiasm.

The shopkeeper did not know the Montana idiom, but she understood the Americans perfectly. With exclamations of *grande, magnifique*, she laid before the critical eyes of the Montana senator a wreath as large as a hoop.

"How much?"

All shopkeepers of all nationalities understand these words. "*Soixante-cinq francs seulment, m'sieur. C'est une vraie occasion*," cried the woman.

Senator Diggle laid a gold piece on the counter and looked at her, solemnly. The shopkeeper held up her hands and protested shrilly. He laid down another very slowly. The shopkeeper simulated tremendous indignation and picked up the wreath to put it back in the window. One after another, he laid down the gold pieces very slowly, pausing enquiringly before each, and sighing most painfully. At last even a French shopkeeper could affect innocency no longer; the stolid face of the woman was lit up by a grim smile, and Senator Diggle carried off his wreath in triumph to the cab.

To hint faintly at the emotions of the senator from Montana as he entered the grand mausoleum, is beyond the power of the writer of this veracious narrative.

For the first time in his life he realized that his boots squeaked and regretted it. He walked about on tip-toe, his hat held behind his back. His mouth was wide open. He shook his head from side to side. He closed his eyes in ecstasy as he counted the battered and torn banners that hung on the chapel.

With his huge wreath dangling on his right arm, he wandered about from one place to another to get different points of view as to where the wreath would prove the most effective. He would have liked to drop it over the circular parapet to the red marble sarcophagus beneath, but the persistent gaze of a gendarme made him feel somewhat uneasy and embarrassed, and vaguely doubtful as to the expediency of so startling a manifestation of regard. At last, after many heart-burnings, he decided to lay his wreath on the steps of the chapel.

He took out one of his visiting cards: Senator Napoleon B. Diggle, Butte, Montana. It was printed in the office of the Butte *Intelligencer*, and was considered by the senator to be a miracle of taste and typographical art. On the top of this card he wrote: "Senator N. Diggle, as a tribute of respect to N. Bonaparte." The unusual abbreviation of the hero's name was not due to any undue presumption on the part of N. Diggle, but merely to the fact that the senator's handwriting, being bold and free, covered too much of the card to permit the writing of both names. On the bottom of the card he wrote: "America to France." This card he tied conspicuously to the wreath and placed the latter on the chancel steps.

Then he stood a little distance apart, and contemplated his offering with a serene satisfaction. He assumed his senatorial attitude—one hand thrust in his breast, the other gracefully resting in the small of his curved back; his torso supported on the left leg. He sunk his chin on his breast and meditated deeply on the decay of greatness. His meditations were rudely interrupted.

"Oh, but I say now, please look at that French chap, will you? What a consummate aws! And that huge wreath, perfectly ridiculous, don't you know. He, he! The sentimentality of these French fellahs is simply disgusting, by Jove. And that pose! 'Pon my word and honor, sir, but the cad was imitating Napoleon. He, he!"

Senator Napoleon B. Diggle drew himself up to his full height of six feet three inches in his stockings, and looked down at the speaker. A diminutive Englishman with a monocle in his left eye was pulling the sleeve of a fellow-countryman, and pointing directly at the hero-worshipper.

The Senator's eyes blazed. His chest heaved. His senatorial pose fell all to pieces.

He, a Frenchman, *he* sentimental! He gnashed his teeth and glared at the traducer. But the diminutive Englishman, overjoyed that his rudeness and malice had proved effective, screwed his monocle in his eye more firmly and deliberately read aloud the inscription on the card:

"'Senator N. Diggle, as a tribute of respect to N. Bonaparte. America to France.' Dear, dear, an American. That fellah is an American. He is a disgrace to his country. I always knew, of course, that Americans were quite impossible, don't you know; beastly cads, by Jove, but really, really, you know,—I—nevah could have im—imagined that they were such awses, *such awses*, don't you know."

The miserable millionaire felt himself turn crimson and then very pale. It was not enough that he be insulted, then. The stars and stripes were to be trailed in the dust no less ignobly. He walked away, digging his nails in the palms of his hands and breathing fiercely. His small tormentor, however, dogged his footsteps like a fox terrier after a lion. Each moment the insults stung more painfully.

"A fellah might think, you know, that these Frenchmen and—*and* Americans had nevah heard of—of Waterloo, by Jove. Now I say, I—I don't see any English flags here, you know. To defeat a handful of Russians and Austrians with overwhelming odds on your side, that sir, I—I declare to be schoolboy play, yes, sir, de—decidedly, sir. Absolutely. Napoleon, sir, I—I protest was no genius. A mere creature of—of happy circumstances, don't you know. Really, a—a puppet in the hands of capricious fortune."

It was enough. The insult to himself he might have passed over; the impudent raillery against the Americans, possibly; but mud thrown at Napoleon?—never. Senator Diggle was not a belligerent man. It took a great deal to arouse him, to make him lose his temper. But when he had lost it, something generally happened.

He had lost it now, and something was going to happen.

Solemnly, very, solemnly, he went out into the blazing sunshine. He walked slowly, very slowly, across the graveled courtyard to the gate. His head was bowed on his breast. He was as one who has a sacred trust committed to him and intends to discharge it faithfully, conscientiously.

At the gate he waited. And not long. Jauntily swinging his cane, quite ignorant of the retribution that was to descend on his guilty head, the slanderer of himself, America, and Napoleon, came strolling, humming "God save the Queen." The air was not such as to appease the Senator's wrath.

Senator Napoleon Diggle buttoned up his frock-coat, and pulled down his cuffs. His wide-brimmed crushed hat he held beneath his arm. He took another of the printed visiting cards from his pocket-book. He had read how these things were done, and he intended to do the thing with due decorum. The heinousness of the offence demanded that.

He presented the card to his foe with gravity. "It is my card, sir," he said, tapping it fiercely.

The diminutive Englishman screwed his monocle in his left eye. "Ah, is it, indeed, me good fellah?" he asked with interest. Then he turned his back on the smoldering wrath of the politician from Butte.

His arm was grasped not too gently. He found himself spun about with a most rude, astonishing, breath-taking agility.

"I said that's my card," cried the Senator threateningly.

"Is it, indeed, me good fellah?" repeated the other uneasily, squirming in the grasp of the giant.

"It is. And what's more, you've got to take back those insults against me and America and Napoleon. Or I'll give you a bigger spanking than your mammy ever gave you with the back of her hair-brush."

The Englishman glanced imploringly towards the mausoleum,[7] then up and down the street. His fellow-countryman was nowhere in sight, and excepting two women drinking at the little café across the wide square, not a person happened to be on the Avenue Trouville.

"But, really, me good fellah, I—I have no insults to retract," cried the enraged little wretch.

"Is that so? Then I guess you take a spanking."

The Senator spoke with a grave, deliberate joy. He tightened his grasp on the others arm; gave his trousers a hitch; heaved a grunt of satisfaction; and before there was any possibility of crying out or attempting escape, he of the monocle was whirled over on the knee of the hero-worshiper after the manner familiar to many of us in our childhood days.

The great hand raised mighty blows on the guilty one to the rhythm of howls of pain and rage. As for Senator Diggle, he wasted no breath in vain words. He uttered deep grunts of anger like a worried boar.

At last, exhausted, but appeased, he hurled his humiliated traducer prostrate in the gutter, and glowered down on him magnificently.

"Me a Frenchy, eh? An aws, did I understand? Sentimental, did you say? You spit on the star spangled banner, do you? Napoleon a puppet of fortune? Oh."

And now for the first time, the doughty Senator became aware of an excited little gendarme dancing frantically around him and brandishing his bayonet and shrieking imprecations and entreaties with equal despair and. volubility.

"*Au nom de la loi, arretez. Arretez, je vous en prie; je vous demande.*"

"And what do *you* want?" asked N. Diggle, at last, looking gloomily down at the shrieking little policeman.

"*Il faut aller chez le commissaire de police.*"

"Eh? Talk like a Christian, you jabbering little spit-fire."

"*Allons, allons. Toute de suite. Allons, je vous en supplie.*"

"He says it's necessary for you to go with him to the station house," said a young American art student, who stood there with his portfolio under his arm. "I say, though, you did give that chap a trouncing. It served the little beast right. He was downright impudent. I heard all he said to you."

The Senator's face brightened. "Thank my stars, there's some one as speaks like a Christian. Must I go with that thing?" He pointed to the anxious little gendarme.

"Yes; you had better go quietly. These French chaps are the deuce for the law. But I will go with you, if you don't mind, and fix up things if I can. My name's Franklin—William Franklin."

The Senator wrung the outstretched hand with gratitude.

And so the procession started for the bureau of police.

With each step the crowd gathered numbers.

The facts of the assault—enormously colored—spread like wildfire. A great statesman from America, some said the President of the United States in disguise, had given the Lord Mayor of London or the first Lord of the Treasury a severe chastisement because the latter had slandered *la belle France* and her heroes. Ah, that was like the noble, the chivalrous Americans. It was to be seen, then, if one could slander *le grand Napoléon* with impunity.

The disgrace of arrest became a march of triumph. Cheers rent the air. There were cries of "*Vive l'Américain! Vive Napoléon! Vive la France!*" The gendarmes, walking deferentially by the side of the hero, smiled genially and hoped that some of the glory fell on their own heads, as the Senator with his hat in his hand, bowed right and left to an admiring constituency.

The arraignment before the commissaire of police was a parody of justice.

When the interpreter repeated the evidence for the plaintiff, the court listened coldly and with a smiling, contemptuous skepticism.

On the contrary, the plea of the defendant called forth great enthusiasm and applause. Senator Diggle did himself justice. In glowing words he sketched the long journey—his Mecca—from the wilds of Montana to the Queen of Cities. He painted the sacredness of that purpose. He emphasized the amazement, nay horror, that he had felt at the blasphemous words, the sacrilege against France and Napoleon. That he was, in a sense, guilty of the assault he did not deny; but he declared that he was ready to uphold Napoleonic ideals at the cost of imprisonment, yes, even of his lifeblood, should that prove necessary. The provocation had been great; he therefore begged the leniency of the court.

Franklin wrung his hand as he sat down and whispered, "Stunning." The gendarmes, the clerks, and the commissaire himself would gladly have embraced him if they had dared.

The commissaire winked a scandalous wink of encouragement to the Senator. Then he whispered to the gendarme who had caused the Senator's arrest. After that, he began to question the officer of the law with blustering severity.

Did the gendarme himself witness the assault? Was there, in short, any assault? If there was, where were the witnesses? If there were no witnesses, what grounds had the officer for presuming to arrest the gentleman?

To all these questions, the gendarme gave most extraordinary answers. He pretended to become very much confused all at once. Certainly he had heard the Englishman calling in a rather louder tone of voice than is generally heard in Paris; and seeing the Englishman seated on the ground and apparently very angry at something, he (the gendarme) had, in the excitement of the moment, stupidly supposed that the tall American gentleman had been the cause of the Englishman's excitement. Very likely it was because the tall American gentleman happened to be standing near by. He believed that there were no witnesses, or if there were, they refused to testify. No doubt his zeal for the law had outrun his discretion. He hoped that the court would not condemn him too harshly for his hasty action.

In reply the court declared that it was both surprised and pained that an officer of the law should be so wanting in discretion and intelligence. Granted that there had been a mere matter of words between two foreigners, did the officer think that so trivial a matter was worthy of the attention of the court? Because an American gentleman happened to be standing near an Englishman who was speaking in a louder tone of voice than is customary in Paris (though not necessarily so in London) was absolutely no reason for subjecting the American gentleman to the indignity of arrest. Clearly interference on the part of the law was quite unnecessary. The prisoner was discharged with apologies for the inconvenience that he had been put to by an over-zealous officer.

Senator Diggle stalked from the courtroom a hero. But he did not pay any heed to the murmurs of admiration that greeted him. He had had enough of *la belle France.* He had upheld Napoleonic ideals. His mission was accomplished. He broke through the applauding crowd, shook the hand of the friendly art student, jumped into a cab and was driven away to his hotel and thence to the Gare de Lyon.

And before night, Senator Napoleon B. Diggle of Butte, Montana, was whirled southwards on his way to wrest fresh laurels from the hand of fortune in hunting the king of beasts in the sandy wilds of Africa.

CHAPTER VIII.

IN BORROWED PLUMES.

IN the meanwhile, quite unconscious of the chivalrous upholding of American honor and Napoleonic ideals on the part of his living namesake, Pennington alighted from the Boulogne express precisely on the same evening that Senator Diggle was departing south to hunt lions.

He was driven to the *Hôtel du Grand Aigle Américain* where he had telegraphed for rooms in advance.

"And the name, if *m'sieur* would be so kind?" asked the concierge, with a subdued air of expectancy. .

Pennington had hoped to have done with the cognomen of Diggle after his landing at Southampton, but the cheque given him by Mrs. Harris (which he had no intention of refusing), made payable to N. B. Diggle, together with the necessity of being identified as such by one of the passengers of the *New York*, whom he knew to be in the same hotel, compelled him to assume a little longer the name which now he most heartily detested. So he answered carelessly:

"Mr. N. B. Diggle of Montana."

The effect was electric. The concierge stared. The guests stared. The porters stared. Everybody stared. As if by magic the name of Diggle was echoed from all quarters. It was repeated excitedly in the office. It floated faintly down from the stairway. It was whispered in the smoking-room.

The concierge darted frantically into the office. The manager darted wildly out. The concierge smirked and bowed. The manager smirked and bowed. Even the guests began to smirk and bow.

Pennington rubbed his nose somewhat embarrassed. "I have heard of French courtesy," he said to himself, "but I should say that for doing the thing artistically, this could not be improved upon."

The concierge led the way to the elevator. The manager placed his hand upon his heart and bowed again. The glory was too great to be borne. Never since the great Grant had blessed the hotel with his distinguished presence, had the house been so greatly honored. But there should be nothing—absolutely nothing left undone to insure monsieur's complete comfort and convenience. Perhaps monsieur wished to avoid the notoriety of public gaze? Monsieur should have dinner served in the private dining-room. And what would monsieur be pleased to drink? If monsieur would only condescend so highly as to leave it to him, he would see that monsieur's dinner should be the very best that Paris could afford. Absolutely. Would monsieur be so kind as to give himself the pains to step on the elevator?" Ah, a thousand thanks.

"The deuce take it," said Pennington, looking about him, after the manager had softly closed the door, "am I dreaming, or is it that Providence, not satisfied with handing me three thousand dollar and two thousand pound cheques, has other prizes in store for me as well? It appears so."

He found himself in a splendid suite of rooms evidently reserved for distinguished guests. The suite comprised a sitting-room, a dining-room, a bedroom with bathroom and dressing-room adjoining. The bed was altogether too magnificent for any head less plebeian than one accustomed to the weight of a crown.

Pennington kicked off his shoes and put on his slippers and smoking-jacket. Then he lit his pipe and threw himself into an arm-chair and wondered what was going to happen next.

The portières separating the sitting-room from the dining-room were noiselessly drawn. For half an hour the subdued rattle of silver and china came faintly to our hero's ears.

At last his curiosity became unendurable. He squinted through the hangings.

Half a dozen men were racing about the room, placing plants here and there and arranging flowers on the table. Silver and cut-glass sparkled.

He sat down again, with a long-drawn whistle. "What in the world am I supposed to be? A duke at least. Perhaps a king." He looked at the shabby smoking-jacket and the slippers, doubtfully. "If I am a king, or even a duke, I can't dine like this. Just what is in the air, Pen, my boy, I don't know; but to the adventurous, adventures come, and we must act up to our rôle."

So he took off the smoking-jacket and kicked off the slippers and arrayed himself in his purple and fine linen.

After an hour and a half's waiting, the portières were drawn aside with a flourish.

"Dinner is served, your Excellency."

His Excellency entered the dining-room slightly abashed, between a row of six waiters. He had seen well-laid tables before, but this one quite dazzled him. He was overwhelmed. And although everything was in perfectly good taste, the decorations were unusual, to say the least.

The American flag hung behind his chair. The French flag faced him. A great shield of magnificent roses, commonly known as *American Beauties*, with the design of the coat-of-arms of Montana worked on it, stood in one corner of the room. In the opposite corner stood a shield of similar dimensions, with the *fleur-de-lis* forming the coat-of-arms of Napoleon. On the walls hung numberless portraits of Napoleon. Busts of Napoleon gazed at him from all corners.

The dinner was in keeping with the decorations. The *carte* informed him that the oysters were served *à l'Américaine*, the soup was *potage à la*

Montana; the fish was *poussin Diggle;* the turkey, *dindon à la Tombeau Napoleon premier.* And during the dessert, a magnificent jelly—the precise resemblance to the sarcophagus of Napoleon—was triumphantly set before him by a blandly smiling waiter.

Pennington ate, drank, and wondered. He sipped his coffee and smoked his panatella[8] with all the sublime insolence of the Sultan or even of the Great Mogul. Still he wondered.

A servant entered with half a dozen cards. "*Messieurs de la presse—les reporters,*" said the man, apologetically.

"Oh, I can't bother with those reporter fellows now," cried Pennington, waving the cards grandly away. "Tell them I have nothing to say to-night, and by Jove, that is the truth," chuckled he to himself.

Another knock. More cards. Mr. Stanley Powers, of the *S. S. New York* begged that he might pay his respects.

"Tell him, please, that I do not feel well enough to see any one to-night. And I say, waiter, won't you bring me several of the papers of yesterday and to-day?"

"*Bien, m'sieur.*"

The papers laid on the table, the door shut, Pennington pounced eagerly upon them. "Now for a solution of this mystery, for mystery there must be. Hum! Nothing out of the way in yesterday's paper." Not yet had the star of Diggle blazed upon the world. Nor was there anything in the papers of the morning. The star of Montana's great statesman was not even then on the ascendant. "Halloa! Creeping snakes and bucking bronchos, what's this?"

The paper fell from his nerveless hand. He flung himself, stunned and prostrate, in the chair.

The episode that had taken place at the tomb of Napoleon was the news of the day. It was allotted to no obscure corner; It headed the first columns of all the evening papers. However much the different accounts varied in details, every newspaper emphasized the senatorial dignity, the wealth, and the chivalry of the gentleman from Montana. The *Journal de Débats* drew an enthusiastic parallel between this unpretentious noble-hearted American, once simple peasant but now millionaire and statesman, and that other great American of days gone by, the printer and diplomat, Benjamin Franklin, whom the proudest court of Europe had delighted to honor. *Le Gaulois* pointed out the intense sympathy that bound all Americans to Frenchmen, and the bitter hate that still existed between the English and their once rebellious colony. *Le Figaro* declared that the affair would do more to cement the friendships of the two great republics than would years of diplomacy. The Paris edition of the *New York Herald* deprecated the affair as indeed unfortunate, but admitted that the gentleman from Montana would be a five-days' hero among Americans and Parisians alike.

So this was the meaning of the extraordinary reception. The Diggle of his fancy actually existed. Perhaps he was walking the streets of Paris that very night, unknown, unhonored, while he, the usurper, the false borrower of a name, was hailed as the public hero, the darling of Americans and Parisians, the lusty vindicator of America's good name and of bright Napoleonic ideals. Hence these busts of Napoleon, hence the sarcophagus jelly, this *poussin Diggle*, this *dindon à le tombeau Napoléon.*

He would explain the ridiculous mistake at once. He pressed the bell and told the servant to call the manager.

Ah, a thousand pardons, but M. le Manager had gone to the Opera. Doubtless he would return soon. Indeed they would fetch him if monsieur wished. Nothing was to be lacking for monsieur's[9] comfort and convenience.

"No; you needn't bother to fetch him, I suppose. It isn't of much importance. To-morrow will do just as well."

"*Oui; Excellence.*"

"And a pleasant task it will be," growled Pennington, flinging the stub of his cigar in the fire. "I am not *the* Senator Diggle of Butte, Montana, if you please, Mr. Manager. I'm only an imaginary senator. I'm only an adventurer. I'm not a hero. I haven't thrashed any Englishman. I haven't had anything to do with this cementing of friendship between France and America. So all this display of sarcophagus jellies and busts of Napoleon are wasted on the desert air. I'm simply Norman B. Pennington, late reporter of the New York *Courier.*"

Pennington gazed moodily in the fire. "No; I am afraid that the explanation of to-morrow won't be pleasant," and he poked the fire viciously.

CHAPTER IX.

I AM NOT WHAT I SEEM TO BE.

THE next morning Pennington glanced somewhat fearfully into the dining-room, dreading lest there should be any more striking features in the floral or gastronomic line, commemorating the heroic episode of the day before.

He was greatly relieved to find nothing more startling awaiting him than a silver tray with coffee and rolls, and a huge batch of French journals. Pennington glanced them through.

"Now if I wasn't so horribly mixed up in this silly affair," thought he, as he sipped his coffee, "I really should enjoy it. The situation is not without it's humor. And these French newspaper men have some ideas of enterprise. Either they have cabled to Butte for the standing of my now notorious name-sake, or they have interviewed some of the American Colony rather thoroughly. A very pretty biography indeed. By Jove, I had no idea that I hit the truth so near the bull's-eye when I amused that kind-hearted Mrs. Harris—Heaven bless her generosity—with all those yarns of mine. It appears that I am quite a fellow. Supposed to be worth at least fifteen million francs, eh? That's a fair income, I should say. And I am well known in Montana as a statesman and public citizen. Very good. *And* a national reputation as a shooter of big game. Hum, let me see. I believe I have fired off a rifle exactly six times in my life. And here is a personal description of myself of course. But not a ghost of a suspicion that I am not the real Diggle—that I am an adventurer, parading about in old Diggy's borrowed plumes. Poor beggar, I suppose he may be gnashing his teeth even now at my rude usurpation of his honors. Well, what have we here?"

"'It was rumored that the American Senator who distinguished himself so nobly yesterday had left Paris last night. One who was an eye-witness of the chastisement of the Englishman is quite certain that he recognized the American Senator as he bought a ticket for Marseilles at the *Gare de Lyon.* We have since proved this to be undoubtedly false. Senator Diggle is the honored guest of the *Hôtel du Grand Aigle Américain*, where doubtless many of his countrymen will call on him during the day. It is rumored that many of our own statesmen will take the liberty of paying their respects informally to the distinguished American statesman.'"

Pennington stretched out his legs and studied the points of his shoes.

"I wonder if Diggle *has* left Paris. If he had, it would explain many things. It would account for his non-appearance on the scene of his honors. Just why he should disappear so suddenly, though, is beyond my imagination. However, I have no intention of robbing poor Dig. of his glory. So now for a little interview with the manager. I am glad that I am used to interviews, especially unpleasant ones. Because this one promises to be decidedly unpleasant."

"I want to see the manager, if he is at liberty," said Pennington, to the servant who answered his call.

"*Oui, m'sieur.*"

The manager appeared, not a little anxious at the summons.

"Ah, pardon, monsieur, a thousand pardons, that I should have been so guilty as to have been out last night, when monsieur wished to see me. That monsieur has complaints quite desolates me."

"M. le manager," began Pennington briskly, though in very bad French, "I am afraid there has been a—how do you call it? slight misunderstanding."

"Ah, pardon, monsieur, I am more than shocked to hear you say so. Every reparation possible shall be made."

"No; no. You do not comprehend, I am afraid. It is I who have unconsciously fallen into error. You seem to imagine that I am Mr. Diggle, the Senator from Montana."

The manager spread wide his hands and bowed. "We have that honor, monsieur."

"And I am sorry to say that I can lay no claim to that honor. I am not the Senator nor am I a millionaire; and I had—I assure you—no hand in the affair that has caused so much excitement and comment."

"As to that monsieur need have no fear. Absolutely none. All France is indebted to monsieur for his magnificent courage in chastising *le bête Anglais* for his disrespect to *la belle France* and her heroes."

"*La belle France* be hanged," muttered Pennington. "But I tell you it was not I who did that," he cried angrily.

The manager smiled with polite skepticism.

"Then would monsieur deign to tell me who he is? Is he not Senator Diggle from Montana?"

"Not the Diggle that you mean. No; certainly not."

The manager wrinkled his eyebrows and looked perplexed.

"And monsieur, did he not telegraph from Boulogne for rooms in the name of M. Diggle of Montana, and did he not inquire for those rooms on his arrival at the hotel?"

Pennington was trapped—very neatly trapped. He frowned despairingly.[10]

"Yes, yes; of course. Only I mean that I am not the Diggle that you mean. There are two of us, it would appear. I'm not the Senator. I'm another man. Quite another man, distinctly so. I'm not the man, don't you see, that flogged the Englishman at the tomb of Napoleon yesterday. I'm a distant relation—his brother-in-law, in short. Happened to bear the same name, don't you know. Very queer coincidence. Just his brother-in-law, that's all. Hardly any relation, you understand."

Pennington wiped the perspiration from his forehead and looked at the manager beseechingly.

A radiant smile broke over that gentleman's wrinkled face. Now it was plain. Perfectly. These Americans were so modest. This queer M. Diggle simply wished to avoid notoriety. It was perfectly clear.

"Ah, I understand. Monsieur wishes to be incognito, is it not so?"

"Yes, yes; just so. Precisely." Pennington clutched desperately at the manager's coat. "Simply to steal away quietly, don't you see? Before there is any comment. No fuss, no silly notoriety, dear Mr. Manager."

The latter's face became very long. That would be disastrous for the hotel indeed. But if he could persuade the American to remain just one day more, then he would take good care to arrange matters that it would be inconvenient, if not impossible, that he leave for two weeks at least. A little judicious lying was alone necessary.

"It shall be kept secret. Absolutely. But no doubt there will be many callers. And the newspapers, you comprehend, monsieur, how inquisitive they are, and they prattle so." The manager shrugged his shoulders deprecatingly.

Pennington stamped his feet. "But I tell you that you must deny the story of the newspapers. It is just that which I insist upon. You *must*, I tell you."

The door opened and Mr. Stanley Powers, one of Pennington's fellow-passengers of the *New York*, pushed his way in followed by an expostulating servant, who was pulling remonstratingly on the gentleman's coat.

"It's all right, I tell you, fellow. The Senator and me are good old acquaintances. My dear Diggle, the chap refused to let me in, confound his impudence. If I hadn't had a little gall, I should have been sent right about face; yes, sir, right about face by a little rat of a Frenchman. You've got to have push, in this world, got to have push, if you'd get along."

"Ah, but monsieur does not wish for publicity," cried the discreet manager to the new arrival.

Pennington turned to his unbidden guest. "Perhaps it's just as well you have come, because I am in a fix."

"In a fix, in a fix, eh?"

"Look here, Mr. Powers, I have been trying to explain to the landlord that I didn't have anything to do with that ridiculous affair of yesterday and the man refuses to believe me."

Mr. Powers laughed immoderately. "Come come, my boy, you are too modest by half. Yes, sir, by half. If you didn't do it, who in the green earth did? That's what I say, who in the green earth did?"

"Precisely," cried the manager, rubbing his hands gleefully.

"Do you suppose that there is only one Diggle in the world? It must have been another Diggle, of course."

Mr. Powers slapped him on the back. "My dear fellow, my dear fellow, that's too delicious. Another ex-cowboy, I suppose? Another millionaire from Montana, eh? And another senator, of course. Come, come, my dear fellow, you are too modest, altogether too modest Ha, ha, ha."

"It is quite possible," said Pennington sulkily.

If Mrs. Sally Harris could have read the mind of her "dear friend N. B. Diggle," at that moment it is doubtful if the said dear friend would have had a cheque for two thousand pounds in his pocket-book.

"But monsieur wishes the matter to be hushed up," interpolated the manager, tapping Mr. Powers on the arm, but secretly rejoiced at the unexpected alliance.

"Hushed up, hushed up, that's good. Why all the Americans in Paris, yes, sir, all the Americans in Paris, are dying to congratulate you, Dig, my boy. You are monarch of all you survey, of all you survey. The hero of Paris. No end of swells were asking for you as I came upstairs. Hushed up, hushed up? Absurd, absurd."

Pennington groaned.

The manager rolled his eyes in ecstasy[3].

"But that would be very disagreeable for M. Diggle," expostulated that arch-hypocrite, solemnly wagging his head.

The humor of the situation broke in on Pennington and he could be angry no longer. Here he was palpably a thief! The thief of another man's name and reputation. He had been caught with his hand accidentally thrust in another man's pocket. He had honestly striven to take it out. But strangely enough, the world insisted in holding it there, and then refused to believe him the thief. Very well, then, let it stay there.

He laughed. "But I say, you can understand how I should dislike all this fuss, you know," he said confidentially to his guest.

"Certainly," echoed the crafty manager.

"Rubbish, man, rubbish. Stuff and nonsense. I wish I had done the thing. It just happens that the affair is the talk of the city, and there is no reason why you shouldn't enjoy fame's little day, yes, sir, enjoy fame's little day."

"Fame's little day may go to blazes," said Pennington crossly.

A servant brought in half a dozen visiting cards. Pennington read them aloud: "M. le duc de Gobelin, M. de Fabrique, Mr. John Ganeswoort Wurst, M. le Chevalier d' Esclande, Mr. Waldorf Astoria."

Delicious shivers ran up and down the manager's spinal column.[11] "Ah, you see, monsieur, all the world demands you. A duke, monsieur; a minister of the interior; the editor of *La Telegraphe;* a member of the

Chambre des Députés."

"And there's Astoria, the millionaire, and Wurst of the American embassy," added Mr. Powers.

Pennington gave a pull at his tie and twirled his mustache. "I suppose you may as well show 'em up, Mr. Manager," he said nonchalantly.

"As monsieur wishes." The manager bowed to the ground.

Mr. Stanley Powers shook our hero warmly by the hand. "You see you are in clover, in clover, my boy. Now, now, don't forget. The West looks to you to do her honor, to do her honor, my boy. Good-morning, Dig., my boy, good-morning."

"Good morning, Mr. Powers," said Pennington with dignity.

"It is too late to retract now, it appears," said he, looking at himself in the glass. He threw out his chest and struck a pose. "For the present, then, I am no longer Norman Bridgworth Pennington, but the illustrious Senator Napoleon B. Diggle in earnest, owner of silver mines galore and a statesman[12] of renown, the picturesque chastiser of the slanderers of *la belle France* and her heroes. Well, to the adventurous, adventures come. Let them come. N. Diggle is ready to meet them—is ready for any adventure, any emergency—even for the real Diggle."

Then his face fell. "And all this is going to costs me a pretty penny."

But as the foot-steps of those who were to do him honor echoed without, he arose, gracious and radiant, to enact the hero for all comers.

CHAPTER X.

'TWIXT THE DEVIL AND THE DEEP SEA.

THE hand on the clock of the Palais Royal had barely passed the hour of ten, when a young man sprang up the steps of the Louvre and entered the main entrance hall as flurriedly as if all the police of Paris were at his heels.

He half ran, half walked, down the long gallery of sculpture and ascended the broad steps of the stairway two at a time; He raced by the Winged Victory as if it had no more interest for him than a brick wall; then, striding down another corridor, he darted out on one of the little balconies that overlook the court yard.

"Whew! What an escape! Again I've escaped the sword of Damocles," he cried, wiping the perspiration from his forehead and leaning on the rail of the balcony quite exhausted. "But when is all this going to end? When *is* the sword of Damocles going to fall? Merciful heavens, when? I'll leave Paris to-night. Yes; *this* time I mean it. I leave Paris to-night. Jove! What an escape! There I was swinging along the Rue de Rivoli. But just outside the Continental I almost tumbled on Willie Franklin—Willie Franklin of all people! One of the artists of the *Courier* not six months ago! But who should he be with but that fellow Wurst of the Embassy, who, of course, knows me as Senator Diggle. Both of them recognized me at the same moment. Willie shouts 'Pennington,' Wurst screams 'Diggle;' I take to my heels. I double back in the gardens of the Tuilleries; skirmish behind some trees; sprint across the courtyard of the Louvre; take refuge in the shrine of art."

"Again I've escaped as by fire. But I take no more chances. Yes; this time I mean it. I leave Paris to-night. But how many times have I already made that resolution? Four times I've packed my trunk; once I even got to the station. But it seems I am fated never to get off. There are always obstacles." He leaned on the rail of the balcony, abandoning himself to gloomy reveries.

But not for long. His reveries were rudely interrupted.

"But by all that's knowable, Wurst, I swear to you that it was Pennington of the *Courier*."

"Pennington of the *Courier!* It was Diggle, I tell you, Senator Diggle. The chap that thrashed the Englishman."

The tall young man started in guilty fear. The voices were so perilously near. The disputants seemed to be below, and bending over the balcony, he could see them gesticulating wildly. He caught at the rail in despair. "Franklin and Wurst," he groaned. "And they are after me." He listened panic-stricken.

"Don't I know Pennington when I see him? Wasn't he on the *Courier* with me not six months ago?"

"And didn't I see the Senator in the box of M. de Fabrique at the Opera not later than last night?"

"Come come, Wurst, be reasonable. Don't I know Senator Diggle, too?" shouted the other. "Quite as well as you.' Yes; better. Did'nt I see him thresh the Englishman with my own eyes? Didn't I go with him to the bureau of police? Didn't I hear him make his great speech? Didn't I shake hands with him when he drove off to the station? I know Pennington and I know the Senator, and I tell you that it was Pennington of the *Courier* that we saw just now."

"Well, don't let us quarrel," said the other contemptuously. "We can soon decide the matter. M. de Fabrique says he came in the Louvre not five minutes since, and he certainly has not gone yet."

"Very well; then let us look for him."

"They have gone," groaned the tall young man on the balcony above. "And they are looking for me. So I haven't escaped after all. Perhaps the sword of Damocles is going to fall now. But not if I can help it."

He pulled his hat over his eyes and walked rapidly down the corridor.

He had safely descended the stairway—was already half way across the gallery of sculpture, when he heard the steps of some one running up behind him. Then his name was called. Attempt at escape was useless. He turned to face the adversary. It was Willie Franklin.

"Why, Willie Franklin. My dear fellow, this *is* a pleasant surprise," cried Pennington, shaking the hand of the art student vigorously.

"Are you quite sure that this is a pleasant surprise? I was beginning to think that you had taken to cutting your old friends," said the art student dubiously.

"What do you mean?" asked Pennington, looking very much hurt.

"That it seems a queer way of showing how pleased you are to see people, when you run away from them."

"Run away?" cried Pennington, with well simulated astonishment,

"Do you mean to insinuate that I have been running away from you?"

"It looked very much like it ten minutes since," said the art, student grimly. "I was walking along with Wurst of the Embassy down the Rue de Rivoli when—"

"Stop a minute. You don't mean to say that it was you who were with Wurst?"

"I don't know who else it could be."

"No wonder, then, you thought I *was* running away from you. Because I was running away, but, as I thought, from Wurst."

"Why in the world should you run away from Wurst?"

Pennington looked at the art student tragically. "Why should I run away from Wurst? I don't think you would ask that if you were in my shoes. That fellow persists in mistaking me for the American duffer who distinguished himself at the Tomb of Napoleon. At first I humored his somewhat unaccountable but harmless illusion for the fun of the thing; but his persistency is beginning to weary me. It is a joke no longer. So now perhaps you know why I ran away from Wurst a few minutes since."

The art student threw back his head and laughed uproariously. "And now I understand why Wurst should be so positive. But I say, I would give anything to see Wurst when he finds out his mistake."

"Wouldn't you like to convince him of it now?" asked Pennington insinuatingly. He was beginning to get a little; nervous lest Wurst should surprise him while he was talking with the art student.

"I should like nothing better," cried Franklin with enthusiasm. "Wurst is upstairs."

"Then supposing that you fetch him. It is rather necessary that I remain here, because I expect someone to go out of that door whom I am waiting for."

As soon as Franklin was out of sight, Pennington broke away for his liberty.

He was walking furiously toward the door, when he bumped into a fastidiously dressed fat little fellow who was bowing elaborately to a young lady. The round little man planted himself indignantly in front of Pennington. "Rustic," he said contemptuously, "there are others in this gallery beside yourself, and if you think you have the sole right of way—why bless my soul, it's Senator Diggle."

"Ah, Wurst, how do? But pardon my haste, I must hurry—"

"Hurry! That seems to have been spurring you on all the morning. I saw you outside the Continental not fifteen minutes ago. I was with that fellow Franklin—you know Franklin?"

"Franklin? Franklin? Hum, who's Franklin?"

"Student, you know, in the Beaux-Arts. A good enough fellow, but obstinate as the deuce. My dear Senator, I want to tell you one of the best jokes you ever heard. He mistakes you for some reporter chap called Peebles or Pendelton or some such fool name. I, of course, insisted that you are Senator Diggle."

"A very good joke, indeed," said Pennington, looking uneasily over his shoulder for the art student, "but you will pardon me if I am rather in a hur—"

"I won't keep you more than two minutes," said Wurst, holding

Pennington by the lapel of his coat, "but I would willingly give two twenties to see that painter fellow's face when he realizes his absurd blunder."

"Wouldn't you like to convince him of it now?" asked Pennington graciously.

"If you could only spare the time—"

"Anything to oblige a friend. And you won't mind if I ask you to let me wait here while you fetch him, because I expect a friend hereabouts presently, and it is necessary that I wait for him."

Wurst was too eager to find Franklin to notice the inconsistency of Pennington's remarks. Smiling broadly, he walked down the gallery to find his friend.

Again our hero ran for his liberty. Already he blessed sunshine was dazzling his eyes, already he espied a cab with its door invitingly open, when:

"*Bon jour, M. le Sénateur, bon jour.*"

Frenzied and heedless, Pennington pushed for the door.

His coat-tails were clutched firmly, authoritatively. "*Ce monsieur-là, il veut vous voir.*"

He wheeled indignantly about. An attendant, still clutching at his coat-tails, was pointing at M. de Fabrique, who greeted him with effusion:

"*Ah, mon ami, quelle bonne chance!* M. Wurst, he tell me he would see you."

"Exactly, monsieur, and I am looking for M. Wurst. I believe he left the Louvre hardly a minute ago."

"*Non, pardon.* You mistake. He ask me to watch for you. There is five minutes that I watch here."

"Precisely. Then he is upstairs. I will find him at once. You will tell him I am looking for him?"

"*Certainement, M. le Sénateur.*"

Again Pennington fled down the long corridor. There must be other exits. But where?

There was no time for deliberation. He turned a corner at random only to find himself in another long gallery. Trusting to find an opening at the end of it, his strides consumed the immense distance.

Far at the end of the gallery, clearly outlined by the crimson drapery that hangs behind it, the Venus de Milo, nobly serene with her vague and divine smile, seemed to be gazing at him mockingly. Perhaps the goddess[13] was anticipating the despair that prostrated Pennington when he dashed into the hall that was dedicated to her.

Because the hall had no exit.

He was feverishly about to retrace his steps, when he heard the voices of the attaché and the art student approaching. He ran frantically back into the hall. Fortunately it was still empty. He crouched furtively behind the statue.

But the voices grew nearer. Detection was more than probable. Was he brought to bay at last? He looked about him in despair. Necessity is the mother of invention. He pulled aside the crimson velvet drapery that hangs on the wall on all sides, and straightening himself flat against the wall, he was quite hidden from view as his enemies entered.

CHAPTER XI.

DAMOCLES' SWORD.

Barely had Pennington concealed himself, when the two unwelcome friends entered the hall.

"No, he isn't here. Perhaps he has stepped outside with that friend he was expecting. But at least, you must confess that you were comically mistaken. Not two minutes since, the senator was convulsed with laughter over your absurd blunder."

"Wurst, your delusion is so obstinately upheld, that I fear for your sanity. Why, man, he was poking fun at your strange aberration, most unmercifully."

"Aberration, sir! Be careful of your words, please."

"Well, credit me with eyes and ears, won't you?"

"And you might give me credit for a little common sense, Mr. Franklin."

"Common sense! Do you pride yourself that you have common sense when a man makes fun of you to your face, and you can't see it?"

"I want to warn you, sir, that your boorish abuse is making me lose my temper."

"And I want to warn you that your smug complacency is making me mad."

"Franklin, you are unbearable."

"Wurst, I won't wound your consummate conceit any more by telling you what I— But here comes that pretty Miss Whitehurst. Perhaps she has seen our man. Good morning Miss Whitehurst, you haven't seen a tall young man with—

"Good morning, Miss Whitehurst," interrupted the attache, "perhaps you have seen Senator—"

"A tall young man," continued the art student, "dressed in a gray suit—"

"With a light mustache," continued Wurst.

"Very likely you know him," added Franklin. "His name—

"Of course you recognize the description, Miss Whitehurst. I need not say that it is Sen—"

"Mr. Pen—"

"You might have enough manners not to interrupt me," cried the attache, turning angrily on the art student.

"I should think that the presence of Miss Whitehurst would at least prevent you from giving way to this scurrilous anger," shouted the art student, hotly.

Miss Whitehurst covered her ears with the palms of her hands.

"Mr. Franklin, Mr. Wurst, how dare you quarrel like two disgraceful school-boys?"

"I am very sorry, Miss Whitehurst, that Mr. Wurst has forgotten himself. But he imagines—"

"I beg your pardon, Miss Whitehurst, for this unexcusable outburst on the part of Mr. Franklin, but it appears that the poor fellow is disqualified for his profession. He is actually becoming color-blind."

"Mr. Franklin, you are to sit down on that seat immediately. And you, Mr. Wurst, on that one. Now, if you will both be good, you may tell me what is the matter."

"The most provoking obstinacy on the part of Mr. Wurst, but he thinks I am silly enough to believe—"

"The whole trouble has arisen, Miss Whitehurst, in my trying to show Mr. Franklin how insanely foolish—"

"Silence! You are actually quarreling after I have expressly told you not to."

The two culprits stared solemnly at each other, glad that there were no witnesses. A religious silence ensued.

"Are you never going to tell me what is the matter?" cried the young lady, after a rather trying pause. "I really cannot wait here all day. Why don't you speak, Mr. Wurst? Please don't look so absurdly demure, Mr. Franklin. You asked me, Mr. Wurst, if I had seen a tall young man—"

"With a gray suit," began the latter, sulkily.

"And a light mustache," added Franklin.

"Called Senator—"

"Norman Bridgworth—"[14] interrupted Franklin.

"No; I've seen no young man with a light mustache, tall, dressed in a gray suit, called Senator Norman Bridgworth,"[14] said Miss Whitehurst, unfolding an easel. "But is that all you were quarreling about? I supposed it to be something dreadful. You are both of you ridiculous men."

"Please, Miss Whitehurst, may I go now?" asked the art student, with mock humility.

"Of course you may go, Mr. Franklin. Please don't be silly. Where. are you going?"

"I'm going to Brittany this afternoon, m'm. I am very sorry that I sha'n't be able to look up my old friend, Pen., and so be deprived of the pleasure of seeing poor Mr. Wurst's discomfiture when he learns of his mistake. But as I have said, I leave for Brittany this afternoon to be gone on a sketching tour for a couple of months."

"It's so nice to have an excuse," said Wurst, sneeringly. "You may rely, however, on my sparing no pains to show up your delusion in its most ridiculous light."

"I never saw such ferocious men in all my life," said Miss Whitehurst, after the art student had gone, without deigning to bid the attaché farewell. "Now, Mr. Wurst, won't you please tell me precisely the reason of your quarreling so dreadfully."

"The reason of our dispute is trivial enough, Miss Whitehurst. But that painter fellow's rudeness annoyed me immeasurably. His conceited assurance is simply colossal. You see, both he and I caught sight of a gentleman at the same instant. But unfortunately, this gentleman disappeared from sight almost immediately. Mr. Franklin persists in maintaining that he is a former reporter called Pendelton or Pendennis or Peebles or some such name. But between you and me, it was Senator Diggle of Montana."

"You don't really mean the senator that all Paris is talking about?"

"He and no other. I am sure of it. And he was in the Louvre not five minutes since."

"Not another word, Mr. Wurst. Perhaps he has not left the building. Oh, I wish to meet him above all things. Won't you *please* look once more for him and if you find him bring him to me?"

"You will be here on my return?"

"Oh certainly. This study of the Venus will take me the greater part of the morning."

Behind the curtain, Pennington shivered. "The greater part of the morning! Merciful heavens! I am to stand here the greater part of the morning."

His estimate of the time was slightly incorrect, however.

The hall was filled with a noisy excursion party. He could feel the curtain sway gently as the people passed to and fro before him." He was vainly endeavoring to make his feet form one straight line against the wall, when he felt an immense weight—rotund, soft, yielding—rest for a brief second against him.

Then he felt it spring suddenly away. Simultaneously, there was a deep, guttural cry of alarm.

"*Ah, Ciel, comme je suis effrayé! C'est un homme. J'en suis bien sûr. Oh, c'est terrible! Oh, c'est épouvantable!*"

"*Hein?*" shouted the guide of the excursion party. "*Qu'avez-vous, madame?* You have fear? Wherefore?"

"*Derrière le rideau. C'est un homme, je vous dis. Oh, c'est terrible! c'est terrible!*"

The curtain was pulled roughly aside. Pennington covered his face with his hands. .

"Ah, ha," cried the guide. "*Un voleur,* eh? A robber. Ah ha, we shall see. Pretty quick. *Vite, appelez un gendarme.*"

There was no time to be lost, if Pennington would escape the ignominy of arrest. "Is Mr. Wurst here?" he cried, lifting his voice high above the chorus of *ah has* and *voilas.*

Receiving no response to his question and seeing the approach of a a gendarme, Pennington cried out again with the energy of despair: "Then is Miss Whitehurst here?"

Miss Whitehurst knocked over her easel in her indignation. "Sir?" she cried.

"I shouldn't dare speak to you, miss," answered Pennington, feeling the blood mount, up to his temples, "only the danger of arrest seems so serious—

"Which you doubtless richly deserve," cried the young lady very much annoyed at his audacity in speaking to her. They would think she were an accomplice.

"—That it is absolutely necessary that Mr. Wurst be found to identify me as Senator Diggle," continued Pennington respectfully but firmly.

Miss Dorothy Whitehurst looked at him incredulously. "You, the Senator! You?"

"Yes; me, miss, if you please," said Pennington, lowering his head guiltily and quite, oblivious of grammar.

"And is it customary for senators to hide behind portières and scare old French ladies—perhaps pick their pockets?"

"You can say nothing too severe. My folly is inexcusable. But I am really not a criminal, you know. I hid behind that curtain to play a joke on Mr. Wurst of the Embassy. If only you would be so kind as to see if Mr. Wurst is still in the building he would prove what I say. But here *is* Mr. Wurst. I shall not have to trouble you. My dear Wurst," cried Pennington to the approaching attaché, "I am in a terrible scrape. I have been arrested."

"Arrested!" echoed the attaché, amazed.

"I am arrested because I hid behind this curtain to play a joke on you. Then before I could get out, this young lady came in and so I was discovered."

"It seems to me to be a very poor joke," said the attaché doubtfully. "However, I will see what I can do with the gendarme."

He placed his card with a ten-franc piece beneath it in the palm of the guardian of the law who had been summoned. After many explanations, the gendarme withdrew with apologies.

"But as I said, it seems a very poor joke," said Wurst severely.

"Very likely," said Pennington flippantly.

"I will explain the joke to you later. But if you would only apologize to the young lady for me. I should be very grateful to you," he whispered.

"You can make your own apologies. Miss Whitehurst, this is Senator Diggle."

Dorothy Whitehurst bowed in a way that was rather depressing to Pennington. "Yes; we have heard much' of you, Mr. Senator," she said.

"Thank you," said Pennington humbly.

"Why should you thank me for that?" asked Dorothy loftily. "There is nothing whatever to thank me for. We cannot help hearing about *notorious* persons in these days. There are so many newspapers."

"I am sorry that you consider me to be a notorious person, Miss Whitehurst, and I am sure if you knew how miserable I am that I should have caused you so much annoyance—"

"You are making a great deal of fuss about a small matter, sir. It is not necessary that you concern yourself so much about me."

"Yes, it is, if you please," said Pennington boldly. "Because I have heard of you, and what I have heard makes me feel quite sure that it is necessary I care very much if I have offended you."

"Oh," gasped Dorothy, looking attentively at this very bold young man.

"And although I should be sorry to cause annoyance to any lady, I am doubly sorry to cause you annoyance, because what I have heard of you makes me anxious to stand well in your opinion."

"You said that before," said Miss Whitehurst, beginning to smile.

"That was because I wished to be emphatic," said Pennington, smiling in his turn.

"But you shouldn't be tautological, you know. I remember that rule distinctly in rhetoric."

"This is a very good rule, perhaps," said the attaché crossly, "but I should like Mr. Diggle to explain to me the joke."

"But before the Senator does that, he will be so good, perhaps, as to fold up my easel for me. I am afraid you have spoilt my mood for sketching," said Dorothy, smiling at Pennington.

"And you aren't angry?" asked he, fumbling with the easel.

"No; but I think you are the funniest Senator, I ever saw. Because you aren't a bit dignified, you know, not one bit. Then you are so original, and so chivalrous. Was the Englishman a *very* big man?"

"Not very big," said Pennington modestly.

"Did he struggle *very* hard?"

"Not so very hard."

"Do you know I am sure I shall like you, Mr. Senator. You are so delightfully original and so little conceited."

"And I shall like you, Miss Whitehurst, because you are so-so—"

"Why do you hesitate? Because you can't think of any nice things to say about me in your turn?"

"No; because I can think of so many nice things to say," said our hero fervently.

"I was perfectly sure that the Senator would be good fun," thought Dorothy complacently, as she led the way down the gallery.

And as Pennington folded up the easel, he said decisively to himself: "I shall not leave Paris after all. To the dickens with Damocles' sword. Now that Franklin is off in Brittany, I can stay here in Paris and carry about Miss Whitehurst's easel and things."

CHAPTER XII.

A GIRL'S A GIRL FOR A' THAT.

My Dearest Daddy: You are a stingy man and I don't love you any more. Here is your own Dorothy, the loveliest, most radiant creature (everybody tells me so but you), who must poke at home pouting in a corner, simply because her cruel papa won't let her have respectable things to wear. And to think that you *promised* me, too. Can't afford it! Preposterous fibber of a papa. I'm sure the bracelet wouldn't cost *half* so much as one of those ugly brick laboratories that you are always giving to that stupid Calvin College. Even mamma says that it's a great bargain; and it would pay—it is I who say this—as a mere business investment. Because the poor Russian princess has to sell the stones at half their value (she says so herself, so it *must* be true), to pay her horrid husband's gambling debts. So you will say *yes*, won't you, cross-patch?

If you don't, I'll do something *dreadful*. I'll marry a nice rich man who won't be so cruel to his Dorothy. I'll marry that nice senator from Montana that everybody is talking about so much. He doesn't hoard up his money like a wicked miser that I know. And I *like* the senator if his name is dreadful. I do *really*. And I have been flirting with him—that's what *everybody* is saying, and it's really outrageous, you know. He is a millionaire and nice-looking. If only his name wasn't Diggle. Mrs. Napoleon Diggle, ugh i If I married him (you see how serious I am) I wonder if he couldn't take my name, or else change his own?

I wonder if you read in the New York newspapers how he first came to be taken up by the people here? About two months ago. A *decidedly* laughable introduction, I think.

You know he gave a poor Englishman a dreadful beating at the Tomb of Napoleon, simply because the Englishman made fun of Napoleon Bonaparte and himself. The French papers praised him for it tremendously, and he awoke to find himself the hero of Paris. But the silliest part of the affair happened a night or two later at the Opera, when M. de Fabrique, a member of the House of Deputies, made his appearance in his box in the company of the American hero. I think M. de Fabrique must have made it known somehow beforehand that the American Senator was to be his guest. Because as soon as they entered the box, the people began to crane their necks around to get a glimpse of the hero. And after the third act, one of the company, in a gown made up of the Stars and Stripes—they say that she was going to America and did it to please the Americans—sang Yankee Doodle amid frantic excitement. Everybody seemed to go crazy. The women waved their handkerchiefs, and the idiotic men stood up and shouted: *Vive l'Américain! Bravo! Vive Napoléon! Viva la France! Viva M. Diggle!* I laughed till the tears came. No enthusiasm could be more deliciously out of place, more wholly gratuitous.

But I *must* say that the American gentleman behaved *beautifully.* He shrunk back in the box in the most alarmed way. Poor fellow. He was as pale as a ghost. I could see him tremble with anger. And he didn't look *a bit* the kind of man that I had supposed him to be. Not at all grizzly and like a cowboy and westerny. Because once he was a cowboy you know, and somehow I always think of all senators—especially Western ones—as being very much whiskered and grizzly. But *my* senator can't be more than twenty-five.

Oh dear, I wish I were an Arch-Buddhist or whatever those Theosophist people call themselves, so that I could fly to New York and make you give me that bracelet. (But after all that would be useless because I suppose an astral body couldn't bring the bracelet back to Paris, could it, sensible old daddy?) If I can't get it—I don't mean the astral body but the *bracelet*—by fair means, you would be sorry, wouldn't you, crosspatch, if I tried to get it by—Senator Diggle? And I really think that he likes me—I *know* it very well. He has followed me *everywhere* since he has been in Paris. Nor is he so *very* bashful. I *think* I could make him propose if I wanted to, and I do want that bracelet very much.

Your loving,

DOROTHY.

P. S.—You are not to think, you know, that I *mean* anything by this nonsensical letter, anything *serious* about that Senator, you sober old daddy. So don't please be worried. I don't believe he could afford to keep a wife if he wanted to; he *actually* spends money easier than I do. And I am quite sure I wouldn't[15] marry anybody with such a horrid name as *Diggle.* I am still your own Dorothy, *fancy-free.*

N. B.—But you mustn't think that the postscript is anything *against* the Senator. Of course he has the money to spend, and I suppose that he has the right to spend it. Only if he *is* a millionaire he seems to spend a *great deal* even for a millionaire. Sometimes he simply *flings* it away.

Yesterday the foolish man must have lost at least twenty-five thousand francs betting on a horse called Napoleon Bonaparte. He must have known that the horse had *absolutely* no chance to win, and I *cannot imagine* why the silly fellow should have risked any money on the animal. But he took the loss as coolly as if he had just given a nickel to a beggar.

CHAPTER XIII.

THE FICKLE TURN OF FORTUNE'S WHEEL.

My Dear Richardson: I wish you would see if there is a berth for me on the *Courier.* Because I am coming home. My little part is played. For two months I have been acting the gilded fool, keeping up the reputation thrust on me of being a millionaire. Well, the rôle was a jolly one, no doubt; and I am not going to grumble. The sport was exciting enough. But twelve thousand dollars doesn't[16] last long at the pace I've set myself.

To-night I have just enough money in my pockets to pay a few outstanding debts (I have paid the larger ones, thank heaven), and to buy a second-class passage for New York. The end came only yesterday, when Napoleon Bonaparte was run at the *Longchamps* races.

The name of the beast will bring a smile to your lips, no doubt. I have written to you more than once how the flogging episode has dogged my wretched footsteps during the whole of the time that I have been here in Paris. Of course you can imagine how the name of the miserable animal was at once linked with the confounded alias of mine that I have made notorious by my folly. Everybody expected the eccentric Montana millionaire to enact again for the amusement of Paris the asinine rôle of worshiper of all things Napoleonic—even of a thing with four legs.

I rose to the occasion and affected immense enthusiasm. I hinted at having thousands at stake. But I had tips, none better—how do we newspaper men get them? that the horse hadn't[17] a ghost of a show with Sir Roger. I needn't tell you that I did not risk much money.

On the day of the race I drove to the track in the jolliest of moods. For not to speak of the satisfaction I felt in having sustained (with no more trouble or expense to myself than numberless winks and nods and smiles) my reputation as a believer in all things Napoleonic, there sat by my side the sweetest, gayest, most bewitching little woman in Paris, the daughter of old Whitehurst, of the banking-house of Whitehurst and Crandal.

I think I never realized before just what a charm that little maid had for me. I know that I felt bitter compunctions, for the first time, that I had been spending money in so idiotic a manner during the last two months, and I determined to be very careful of what I had left. If necessary, I would leave Paris, that I might break away from all Diggle ties and Napoleonic obligations forever.

I suppose that while I was thinking of all this I must have been rather glum.

"A penny for your thoughts, Mr. Senator," she cried.

"Oh, I was simply wondering what my chances are on Napoleon Bonaparte," I answered smiling.

"Have you very much money on him?" she asked.

I smiled knowingly.

"Is it very much?" she insisted.

"Perhaps not *very* much according to some people's ideas. It depends on how much *very much* means." I looked steadily ahead with the face of a sphinx.

She pouted. "It seems queer that you should be so reluctant to tell me."

"Very likely," I assented cheerfully.

She frowned. "I think it must be that you have so little on the horse that you are ashamed to tell me. Sometimes I think you are simply pretending to care so much about Napoleon. I question very seriously whether you really do care a five centime piece about the man Napoleon or the horse Napoleon."

"Then why did I flog the Englishman?" I asked coolly.

She made a gesture of impatience. "Ah, there it is again. The flogging of that Englishman! We shall never hear the last of it, I suppose. But the reason for that mock-heroic achievement is easily enough accounted for, isn't it? Did that not first bring you into prominence?"

I shifted my position uneasily.

She grew more confident as she perceived my embarrassment.

"For my part, I have never for a moment imagined that you really were in earnest in your ridiculous devotion. Certainly you have not been at all consistent. Mr. Wurst of the embassy told me himself, that once when he twitted you on your mania for things Napoleonic, you said very angrily, Napoleon be something or other very naughty indeed."

"But Wurst and some other people push things to such extremes," I protested.

She was quite confident now. "Why should you *pretend* to care, just because people expect you to. That is to be insincere, to be playing a part. And to be playing a part falls very short of being an adventurer, does it not?"

Richardson, I tell you, old fellow, if she had struck me with her glove in the face, I should have felt less surprise and consternation.

The blood rushed to my face and almost blinded me, so that I very nearly drove over an old apple-woman. Unconsciously she had told the truth. I saw myself in my true colors. The sight was not pretty.

Presently, when I was sure of myself, I asked her so quietly that I scarcely knew my own voice: "How much do you consider that I should have up, Miss Whitehurst, to persuade you that I believe not only in the man Napoleon, but in the horse Napoleon?"

The question seemed inevitable after what she had said.

She sat there wrinkling up her eyebrows, with an inscrutable little smile of triumph on her lips. Then she tossed her head gaily and declared: "You might possibly persuade me that you are in earnest if you have placed —say, fifteen thousand francs on the horse."

"Now, Richardson, I had precisely twenty-seven thousand, two hundred and fifty francs left out of the seventy thousand francs with which I had come to Paris two months ago. I whipped up the off horse and said quietly: "I shall make fifty thousand francs, Miss Whitehurst, if Napoleon Bonaparte wins." The odds, you are to understand, were two to one on Sir Roger.

Of course I had no trouble in putting up the money at the track. And of course I lost it. That was a foregone conclusion. But no one, least of all Dorothy, I mean Miss Whitehurst, knew that the loss of that money left me literally penniless. The girl has hastened my downfall, a little quicker than need have been, perhaps; and Richardson, dear old fellow, I love her. I love her. But I have found it out when it's too late, it seems. Well, so much the worse for me. But I won't drivel.

I say, do you think you could get me the book reviews or the dramatic column on the *Courier?* The latter would be just the thing. I should get the chance then to study the practicalities of stagecraft, I could easily live on fifteen dollars a week, and I should have the time to work on the Great Play. You know I promised that to the Great Unknown who gave me the three thousand. I don't know whether to curse him or not. At any rate I have promised to write a play. That promise has been forgotten of late. It is time I get to work. So I shall see you in a couple of weeks.

Faithfully yours, old chap,

NORMAN B. PENNINGTON.

(*alias* Napoleon B. Diggle.)

CHAPTER XIV.

"I WILL ROAR GENTLY."

PENNINGTON sat in his shirt sleeves, staring gloomily at two half-packed trunks. The packing of them had been heart-breaking work, not only to the flesh, but to the spirit. He was about to return to New York after an absence of hardly two months—absolutely penniless. The fine linen that he had packed away seemed a great mockery.

But all other regrets vanished into thin air when he thought of the girl he had begun to love. "Ah, that hurts most!" he cried, slamming down the cover of one of the trunks and locking it. "And worst of all, I must see her once more before I leave the scenes of my great folly. I wish I could go to her and confess all. And I would, if she had not unconsciously completed my ruin by compelling me to put up and lose the twenty thousand francs yesterday.

"Just when I had determined to play the fool no more. That's like fate. It doesn't give a fellow half a chance. It is quite impossible that I give her any hint of the part that she has played in my little comedy, and if I told her anything of the truth, she would readily guess that. So silence is inevitable. I don't want to grow sentimental, but it does seem hard on a fellow that he must slink off like any thief, and leave no one behind to explain things.

"However, I can drop the name of Diggle at last, confound him. I can be Pennington once more, though penniless. But that's a vile pun."

He tore out of his card-case half a dozen visiting cards with the name, Senator Napoleon B. Diggle, engraved on them, and flinging them in the fire, stuffed a few of his own in.

"Ah, Diggle, Diggle, if I could get hold of you now, I would take the liberty of giving you a little of my mind. There was a time when I might have been reluctant to meet you. But now, um!"

He began to lace up his shoes. The shoelace broke and he said, succinctly and impressively, "Hang Diggle!"

A knock at the door. "Some one wishes to see monsieur," said the servant.

"Tell the some one that I am sick. Tell him I'm dead. Tell him I'm crazy. I can see no one."

Pennington tore out the broken lace, savagely, and began to hunt for another.

Again a knock. "The gentleman says that his business is most pressing. Quite unavoidable. If monsieur would deign "And I tell you, I won't deign," cried Pennington, angrily, continuing the search, slamming drawers and throwing aside all the chairs and tables that stood in his way.

"The gentleman is most persistent. He says that if *m'sieur* would have the goodness to look at his card, perhaps *m'sieur* might possibly spare a moment to see him." The servant held out the card timidly.

"Bring it here, fellow," shouted Pennington, exasperated. He remembered that he had packed the shoe-laces in the bottom of the strapped trunk.

His nerves were as good as those of most young fellows of twenty-five, but he sprang up as he read the name on the card.

It was a cheap bit of pasteboard, and the name was not engraved. But he studied the card with a profound astonishment. "Napoleon B. Diggle, Butte, Montana," it read.

"Show him up," said Pennington at last with a desperate calmness.

He did not put on his coat. He had no intention of being unnecessarily polite. A month ago the interview might have proved not too desirable. Now he welcomed it with a grim joy.

He unstrapped the trunks and began to toss out the things in search of the laces.

The door opened abruptly. Senator Diggle walked in without knocking. Evidently he, too, had no intention of being more courteous than is considered necessary. He stood in front of Pennington, glaring down at him menacingly.

Pennington did not take the trouble to look up, but he said: "May I ask you to step a little to one side? You are in the light."

The irate senator thumped his clenched list on the cover of the trunk. "Look at me, young chap, and answer me. Are you the scamp that has been calling himself Diggle during the past two months?"

Pennington lifted out a tray very carefully.

"I am not a scamp, neither is my name Diggle," he answered contemptuously.

Napoleon Bonaparte Diggle folded his arms. "Don't tell lies now. Do you mean to deny that you have been known here in Paris by the name engraved on that card?"

He tapped it threateningly just as he had tapped it when he had threshed the Englishman. He believed the gesture had been effective then, and he intended that it should be no less effective now.

"I do not deny that I have been known here in Paris by the name *printed* on that card."

"And do you have the impudence to claim that name for yourself here before my face?"

"If I have claimed the name behind your back I certainly should not disclaim it before your face," answered Pennington, coolly.

"Now then; none of that beating about the bush. You can't fool me that way. I ask you for the last time if you deny that you have been using my name?"

"Do you think it is quite imperative that you shout so? It must be very fatiguing to you and it is rather trying on me, you know."

Senator Diggle gulped indignantly. "You are a scamp, sir; an adventurer."

Pennington looked up angrily. "Be careful what you are saying, please."

"I say-it again; you are an adventurer. Do you think you are going to awe me with your high and mighty airs? Do you think I have never seen a dude before? Do you know who you have to deal with? Do you know who I am?"

"I have heard it said that you are a person who has more money than brains or breeding. Please correct me if I am wrong."

The senator lowered his head like a charging bull. "Well, never mind who I am for the present. It is enough for *you* to know that I have come all the way from Africa to make you get down on your knees and be a little more humble. I am going to make you squirm."

"Are you really? How nice of you. It's so nice to be nice. But, please, don't hurt my poor trunk. It cost me twenty dollars."

"And if you don't, I am going to lay the whip on your shoulders."

"Indeed! How Napoleonic! How Diggletonain! But, my dear senator, please pardon the liberty, but are you quite sure that you can do it? I am not an Englishman, unfortunately, who is decidedly smaller than yourself. I am sorry for it, but I don't think I can oblige you with a squirm to-day."

The senator slammed down the cover of the trunk and crushed in Pennington's hat. "Come now, answer me. What have you to say for yourself? This is your last chance."

Pennington rose slowly to his feet. He resented the crushing of his Dunlap, decidedly.

"What have I to say? Very little, I believe, except that you are a consummate ass, and I have a great mind to give you a flogging for your impudence."

"*Flog* me, sir?"

"Yes; flog *you*," answered Pennington, walking up to the astonished Diggle and standing close in front of him with his hands in his pockets. "Have you not given me provocation enough?"

"*Provocation!*" gasped the senator. "What are you talking about?"

"That is my word, sir, 'provocation.'"

"Provocation! Provocation, you young idiot! Provocation for what?"

"For what! How *dare* you to ask? Because you are insolent in the first place. Because it was not enough that you should play the fool yourself, but you must make it inevitable that I also play the fool."

"I—make—you—play—the—fool?"

"So I said, sir. Was it not enough that you should make yourself the laughing-stock of the world by threshing a small Englishman on the most absurd pretext, without your sneaking meanly off leaving me, who unfortunately happens to have the same name as yourself, to bear the brunt of the disgrace and the penalty."

The senator made one more effort to resume his blustering aggressiveness. "Come, come, now. You talk like a crazy Mugwump with your disgrace and your penalty."

"Disgrace and the penalty. So I choose to construe it," answered Pennington, coolly, sitting down on the trunk. "And instead of thanking me, you threaten to lay the horse-whip on my shoulders. Oh, oh! I never dreamed of such impertinence, not to speak of ingratitude."

"Disgrace! Penalty! Thank you! Ingratitude!" echoed the dazed senator.

"Certainly. Because you are vain enough to call ridicule flattery, and the mock-heroic the heroic—that does not alter the facts, I suppose. I no less deserve your gratitude."

"Eh?" feebly ejaculated the subdued politician from Butte.

"I said I should deserve your gratitude, your gratitude, sir. I believe I am not obscure. Answer me, if you please. Have I belied your reputation as an upholder of Napoleonic ideals? Have I in any way proved traitor to the trust rudely imposed upon me, but none the less sacredly, religiously guarded, of sustaining your character as a hero, as a chastiser of Napoleon's traducers? Have I besmirched Senator Diggle's good name? Answer me, if you please. I insist that you answer me. As for the *expense* of it all, I scorn to mention that."

"Expense," mechanically echoed the other, quite bewildered.

"Yes, sir, I believe I said expense," continued the ruthless Pennington, beginning to imagine himself a very ill-used man indeed. "Perhaps *you* think it costs nothing to be a public hero. Perhaps you imagine that you can always be planted on a pedestal before the dazzled eyes of the world as a hero, as an upholder of Napoleonic ideals, and be at no expense. And while you are reclining on flowery beds of ease in Africa, I, your servant, your understudy, am working like a beast of burden, and spending thousands of francs to fan *your* glory into a radiant flame."

Senator Diggle pushed further up his sleeve a short mule-whip that he had been flourishing a moment before. "Well, it hadn't just struck, me that way," he confessed.

"Very likely not. But please understand that it has struck *me* to the amount of seventy-thousand francs in precisely two months. And then to be insulted. Oh, it's maddening, outrageous! Come, sir, oblige me, if you please, by leaving the room before my temper gets the better of me. I am a long-suffering man, sir, but my patience has its limits."

Was that the stalwart chastiser of Napoleon's traducers? Was that the gentleman, who, scarcely two months ago, had electrified an admiring House, as he set forth in impassioned speech, the glories of his far-distant Mecca?—that feeble, stumbling, unmanly creature, who, with head bowed humbly to the ground, began to slink towards the door?

Half-way across the room, he hesitated. "Mr. Diggle, sir, I guess I was pretty rash and—"

Pennington looked up. "Ah ha, so you begin to see yourself in your true colors at last, do you? You confess to your ingratitude?"

"Well, you see, sir, it hadn't kinder struck me that way."

"Ahem. And—er—what are you going to do about it?"

"I have just come from Africa, where I was going to shoot lions, and I guess I'd better go back again."

"What? And leave me here, still to be your servant, to continue as your understudy?"

"If it wouldn't be too much bother, sir."

"No, no, impossible; impossible, I say. I leave Paris tomorrow. Do you suppose I find it agreeable to do favors to be insulted in return? No, no; I leave you a clear field. You may take my place, and of course people won't think you are an imposter—oh, no. Doubtless you will sustain the part I have created with credit; you have the grace, the polish, the wit!"

"I wouldn't stay here for a nomination to the presidency," said the senator, beginning to look alarmed at the mere possibility of the thing. "I don't know a word of their lingo."

"But to run off, will be quite as bad—worse! Why, think a minute, Diggle. Won't it seem rather queer for the great Montana millionaire to disappear all at once like a thief in the night?"

The senator felt vaguely that it would look very queer indeed.

"If you would only stay, sir," he said, humbly.

"Not a day, not an hour."

"If you please, sir."

"Not an hour, I tell you. I can't afford it."

"How much would it cost, sir, "to do up the thing brown for six months more?"

"Oh, a great deal of money."

"Five thousand dollars?"

"Pooh, pooh, man. You couldn't touch it for that. I flung away that amount only yesterday backing the horse Napoleon Bonaparte."

"Ten thousand?"

"No, not for twenty thousand. If you had shown common decency, if you had come respectfully and said: 'Mr. Diggle, I realize that I am not blessed with that pleasing exterior and grace of manner that would enable me to fan into a flame of splendor the feeble spark of renown that I was the accidental means of igniting. You have done me incalculable service. You have made a deathless reputation for me in Montana, thus making it possible for me to be nominated for governor. (You know that is true, Diggle. I have read the papers). I can never repay you for the service. Money cannot approximate it. But since you are, so to speak, fighting my campaign; and since campaigns do cost money—here is a cheque for twenty-five thousand for present expenses.' If you had come to me thus, I might possibly have listened to you. But to attempt to bully and to, bluster! To threaten to thresh me! It's beyond belief. It was despicable. That Senator, was boorish indeed."

"I will write you out a cheque for twenty-five thousand this very minute," cried the Senator, fumbling in his breast-pocket for his cheque-book.

Pennington shook his head. "No. Nothing can induce me to stay now. You have made your bed. You must lie in it. You must say to Paris, to America, to' the whole World: 'It was not I who so graciously upheld Napoleonic ideals. It was another. *I* am a mere adventurer.' You cannot run for governor. You must retire from the world, Diggle. You had better let the lions devour you."

The, Senator mopped his forehead frantically. "Tell me what I can do to make up for my ingratitude," he cried, seizing Pennington's hand.

"Well Diggle, I believe you to be humble. You have *squirmed* enough. And since you have apologized and are penitent, I will relent to a degree. I cannot stay in Paris. Your reproaches and insinuations have wounded me too deeply for that. But I will give it out before I leave here that *I* am going to Africa to shoot lions. So the world need never know that you were here; need not know that you were not the real hero; that you were only an adventurer."

"Sir, that is indeed magnanimous."

"I do not deny," replied Pennington modestly, "that I have heaped coals of fire on your head."

"I should like to have my benefactor's address," said the Senator earnestly.

"With pleasure, Diggle. Anything that you address to Norman B. Pennington, care of the *Courier*, New York, will reach me."

"N. B. Diggle, care of Norman B. Pennington, New York *Courier*," repeated the other writing the words in his note-book.

"Well, Senator, you may as well scratch out the Diggle. It gives one a pang, no doubt, to discard one's name. But I cannot run the risk of this unpleasant notoriety making me unhappy over there in America. Besides, I wish to make your obligation to me complete. I wish *you* to assume all the glory. And if there were two Diggles, you see, it might embarrass you. I assume the name of N. B. Pennington from to-day. I begin the world afresh."

"That is a great and noble sacrifice, sir, and I honor you." But the Senator struck out the Diggle with alacrity.

"And now, Senator, good-day and good-bye. And permit me to express the hope that should we ever meet again, I shall find you less hasty in your surmises, more considerate, more grateful."

Senator Napoleon Bonaparte Diggle of Butte, Montana, wrung Pennington's hand with an emotion too deep for utterance.

Then he went slowly down stairs on his way to Africa to shoot lions.

Again Pennington began to toss the things out of the trunk in search of the shoe-laces. "I never realized until to-night," he mused, "that I had been doing Diggle such a service."

CHAPTER XV.

LOVERS RUN INTO STRANGE CAPERS.

PENNINGTON walked slowly up the *Avenue de Friedland* till he came to the *Arc de Triomphe.* Then he turned southward down the *Champs Elysées* as far as the *Avenue de l'Alma.* A few steps up that aristocratic street, and he found himself opposite the house occupied by Mrs. Whitehurst and her daughter.

More than once he passed it by with a strange sinking at his heart. It was not that he was nervous, or that much could possibly be at issue because of the call; since any understanding must be impossible under the circumstances. But, naturally, he was more than reluctant to bid farewell to her for probably the greater part of a year.

So much might happen in a year. How to arrange matters that she would permit nothing to happen during the time, to let her understand how much he desired that, without his making this wish deliberately known to her—such was the problem. It was simply the solution of this problem that made him hesitate.

But advancing the third time towards the house, he saw Dorothy looking down the Avenue through the open window.

He rang the bell. "Miss Whitehurst is at home, I believe? Please take up my card and ask her if she will see me." He walked into the reception room.

In a minute or two, the servant asked him to go up into the drawing-room.

Dorothy was standing in the middle of the room, holding his card and looking expectantly towards the door. She laughed when Pennington entered.

"You seem decidedly amused to see me, Miss Whitehurst," he said, somewhat piqued at the laugh.

"Not to see *you*, Mr. Senator, but I did not know before that *this* was your name," she replied gaily, glancing at the card that she held in her hands.

"You don't know my name, Miss Whitehurst, and I have had the pleasure of your acquaintance the past two months."

"Certainly I know your name, or rather I *thought* I did," she retorted. "But perhaps you will agree with me that there is a seeming disparity between Mr. Napoleon B. Diggle of Montana and Mr. Norman Bridgworth Pennington. Which name do you prefer to be known by this afternoon?"

Pennington bit his lip. What an absurd blunder! He had quite forgotten that he had substituted his own cards for those of Diggle. Then he laughed in a rather silly way. "Ha, ha, I do not wonder that, you are surprised, Miss Whitehurst. The joke is on me. So I gave you one of old Pen's cards by mistake. Very funny, he, he. Very silly."

She looked at him suspiciously. "You certainly did, Mr. Senator, or Mr. Somebody Else."

Pennington regained his self-possession. He glanced swiftly at her, askance. Could she possibly suspect?

"You seem to take great pleasure in doubting my word, Miss

Whitehurst," he said in an injured tone. "Yesterday it was my sincerity concerning the horse Napoleon; to-day, because I give you one of my friend's cards by mistake."

"Oh, you take my little joke quite too seriously, Mr. Senator," cried Dorothy, laughing.

Pennington breathed freely again. She did not suspect.

"The mistake was a natural one," he resumed with dignity. "You see it happened that old Pen. (queer old chap is Pen.) happened, just happened, you know, most natural thing in the world, to have left one of his cards around, and I—er—must evidently have put his card in my case by mistake, don't you see?"

"Please say no more,"said Dorothy politely. "It is perfectly clear. But what a nice name, Norman Bridgworth Pennington. Is he himself no less nice, Mr. Senator?"

"Oh, a splendid fellow," cried Pennington, with enthusiasm. "Charming, clever, extremely. Bound to make his way if he only works. Of very good family—the old Pennington stock, you know. Nice fellow in the main."

"I think I have heard of the Penningtons. They are a New York family, are they not? But I believe I have not met your friend."

"Perhaps not. Very likely not. The old chap isn't likely to move in your circle. Unfortunately he has one thing against him."

"And what is that, Mr. Senator?" asked Dorothy anxiously. "Do you know I feel strangely interested in your friend?"

"He is poor, the dear old chap."

"Why, that is nothing against him, Senator Diggle. I am disappointed that you should be purse-proud enough to hint at such a thing being against one. I hardly expected that of you." Dorothy spoke with asperity.

"My dear Miss Whitehurst, I do not wish you to imagine for a moment that I thought his poverty to be against him. Personally, he is the dearest fellow in the world—one of my best friends—I may say my *very* best friend. I love him as myself. I was looking at him simply as a marriageable man."

"And are poor men not marriageable?" cried Dorothy, indignantly. "I declare Mr. Senator, I am afraid that your wealth makes your standards worldly."

"But he has absolutely no social position," protested Pennington, with apparent warmth, but secretly overjoyed at Dorothy's indignation.

"Social position! Poor fellow! But my dear Senator, we cannot all be so fortunate as yourself in that respect. We cannot all be senators."

Pennington flushed. "You are pleased to be rather sarcastic, Miss Whitehurst."

"I am afraid I was rude," she answered, looking at him contritely. "Only in speaking so, you hurt me dreadfully. I am really a little disappointed in you. I supposed that you, at least, would be above that."

"I was simply trying to look at dear old Pen. with the hypercritical eyes of the young ladies' relatives, you see."

"Young ladies' relatives? You imply that he is engaged to a young woman whose relatives object to him?"

"No; he is not engaged; but he would very much like to be."

"Then why is he not? I trust I am not presuming."

"Ah, you forget, Miss Whitehurst. The young lady is so much above him, financially and socially. The poor old fellow doesn't dare to ask her, I am afraid."

"Afraid to ask her! I begin to lose interest in him. He is something of a coward, I fear. I love intrepid men. Your friend cannot be interesting in spite of his nice name. You will not think me rude if I ask his business or profession?"

"He was a reporter on the New York *Courier*. But a few months since, an unknown friend who seemed to believe in him gave him a little money that he might make something of himself."

"How interesting! And is he *going* to make something of himself? I do hope something nice."

"He hoped to write a play."

"Write a play! Oh, how splendid! I did him an injustice in saying that I feared that he must be uninteresting. I do adore those clever literary men. You and I, Mr. Senator, we are the stupid people. Our lives run so stagnantly along. There is positively no excitement in them, no change."

"Just so," agreed Pennington, but thinking far otherwise.

"Now you will grow dull and heavy while making dry old laws that people will insist on breaking. You will be always planning how you may add a few more thousands to a sum already so large that you fling away twenty-five thousand francs just to gratify an idle whim. And I, *I* spend all my time and money on dress-makers and milliners. It is horrid! Do you think Mr. Pennington (it is such a nice name—it sounds so clever—I am in love with him already) do you think that he will succeed? I shall be sorry if he does not. Does he work hard?"

"I am afraid not," said Pennington gloomily, tracing out the pattern of the rug with the point of his shoe. "He has already done some very foolish things. Instead of working hard, he has been gadding about, wasting the money that was entrusted to him."

"No doubt the temptation was great, poor fellow. Did you not say that he was not well off before his friend assisted him?"

"Yes, he had lived on about twenty dollars a week. But that was no excuse. I am disgusted with him. I have almost given him up."

"Oh, but, *poor* fellow, if he had so little money before, the temptation must have been very great," said Dorothy, softly.

"Yes, that is true, and he had not then met the girl he now loves," said Pennington, lifting his head. "But, really, you seem to take a great interest in him."

"You compel me to take his part. You are so bitter and uncharitable. I truly believe that you are jealous of him," she added, quizzingly.

Pennington could not help smiling. Jealous of his own name!

"No, no. That is absurd, Miss Whitehurst," he protested.

"Not at all. You are jealous. Now,I can see it plainly. You are piqued because I included you among the stupid and ordinary people and because I said *his* name sounded nice."

"Then you imply that my name is not nice."

"Oh, by no means," cried Dorothy. "But nevertheless, I believe you to be jealous, morbidly jealous, Mr. Senator."

"Jealous! Miss Whitehurst, jealous of what, if you please? The fellow has done nothing that I should be jealous of."

"The fellow! Done nothing! You are tremendously contemptuous, Mr. Senator. I wonder if all those protestations of friendship for 'dear old Pen,' were quite sincere?"

"To be sure they were," cried Pennington with emphasis.

"And you are still good friends? You have not quarrelled?"

"Impossible! might as well quarrel with myself."

"Then you must be good friends indeed. Tell me, then, is he in America still?"

Pennington shook his head.

"Abroad?"

Pennington nodded.

"Perhaps in Paris?"

"Yes," admitted Pennington, hesitatingly. He had no sooner said the words, than he foresaw embarrassment ahead.

Dorothy leaned forward and smiled engagingly.

"Then, my dear Mr. Senator, you will do me a great favor? Bring him to see me."

She sunk back in the depths of her chair, still smiling at him provokingly. It was such fun to tease the senator! Could one have believed him to be so jealous? Not that she was displeased. By no means.

Pennington was too startled to choose his words. "Oh, but I couldn't possibly do that, you know," he cried, dismayed.

"Do I ask so great a favor? I have never met a playwright," she pouted.

Pennington walked up and down the room in his perplexity. "I must see if I can manage it. But really, I am afraid I can't. I should like to of all things, but I cannot very well. No great obstacle, you know, but it would be so inconvenient, so much trouble, so—" He looked at Dorothy imploringly.

"Please pardon my persistency. I do not wish to cause you trouble. If it is inconvenient—"

"Not at all. Of course not. Trouble? Absurd! Easiest thing in the world, but—"

"You do not wish to?"

"Immensely. I should er—"

"I have been very rude in asking you. I think I can guess at your reason. Mr. Penning ton perhaps is—ah—not quite—ah—is not such as—"

"The fact is, Miss Whitehurst, the fellow is so—so—so very *bashful*. The poor beggar can't go anywhere he is *so bashful*."

"Mr. Senator, you are not frank. You awaken my curiosity and then you refuse to gratify me. That is neither kind nor courteous. But if he is only bashful, I shall insist. No one is bashful with me."

Driven at bay. Pennington said desperately: "The fact is, I am going away from Paris, almost immediately, and I have come to say good-bye."

"Going away! Going away!"

The disappointment expressed in the quavering repetition of the words set Pennington's heart thumping joyously. And he answered almost cheerfully; "Yes; I am going back to America. It is necessary —absolutely necessary."

"I—we—we shall miss you, I fear," Dorothy replied in a troubled voice. "Somehow I—we had not thought of your leaving us—that is—not so soon."

"Miss Whitehurst, I thank you for saying that. I am glad that you will miss me, Miss Dorothy," he said, fervently.

"Then—then why should you go away?"

"Because—"

"Yes, because—"

"Because—"

"Yes, Mr. Senator, because—"

"Well, because I—oh, really, I can't tell you, Miss Whitehurst."

"*Please*, Mr, Senator."

"You will laugh at me."

"No; I shall not."

"It is because I am in love."

Dorothy blushed. "In love, Mr. Senator. How delicious!"

"But if she doesn't love me?" said Pennington, looking out of the window.

"You mean, that is, *do* you mean that you are disappointed in love?" she asked anxiously.

"Hardly that. The fact is, er—"

"Yes; the fact is, er—"

"That I—"

"A little courage, Mr. Senator. You are not afraid of me are you?"

Pennington looked at her adoringly. "Not very much. But if you want to know: I haven't asked her yet."

Dorothy smiled delightedly in his face. "You delicious man. Then why don't you ask her, you foolish Mr. Senator?"

"I don't dare to. I cannot," he answered in a low voice.

She leaned over close to him. "That is very cowardly—very. I declare I am afraid you are no more brave than your friend. To go away because you are in love and then not to ask the young lady. That is funny. Yes; no doubt you are a coward, Mr. Senator. I am disappointed in you. I like intrepid men."

"There are reasons that make it very necessary that I should not ask her. Believe me. It is quite impossible to tell her that I love her, for the greater part of a year. It seems strange enough for me to say so, no doubt. But do you think, Miss Whitehurst—do you think, dear Miss Dorothy, that she would be willing to wait so long?"

"So long for what?" asked Dorothy, looking down demurely.

"For me to ask her."

"Wait so long? Let me see now. It is to be presumed that the young woman is in love with you? You have observed her symptoms?" asked Dorothy with a brisk, professional air.

"I'm afraid she hasn't any; at least she hasn't shown any. She is too proud for that."

"Oh but she has. I mean that she *must* have. They all have their symptoms," said Dorothy, very decidedly.

"No; not a blessed symptom."

"Perhaps you are not observing. Surely she has given you some *little* hint that she is not indifferent to you."

Pennington shook his head gloomily.

"Then how *can* you tell that she cares for you at all?" cried Dorothy, provoked at his obtuseness.

"I can't tell. I suppose. I can only hope."

"Have you ever hinted to her that you care for her?"

"I don't think I have in so many words."

Dorothy pursed up her lips. "Then how is she to know that you care for her?"

"I don't know," said Pennington despondently. "But I supposed that in some way—that there was some way they had—I mean that somehow girls can always tell that."

"I question it very much, Mr. Senator," answered Dorothy coolly. "It a matter of conjecture if she will give you two thoughts under those circumstances. Men are so conceited; they provoke me. They imagine that the young women fall in love long before the men care for them; and they think the girls are unselfishly willing to wait like ripe plums till the men choose to pick them. But the men should remember that there are not so very many nice plums," added Dorothy, looking at Pennington significantly. _

"But if it were quite impossible," protested he. "Supposing I couldn't pick the plums—supposing it was against the law—supposing I were not tall enough and had to grow some more."

"It is never impossible." Dorothy ignored the metaphor. "It doesn't seem to me that it is ever impossible for an honest man to tell a girl that he loves her. If he pretends that it is, he is to be shunned; he is not what he should be."

Pennington twisted his handkerchief into a knot.

Dorothy continued sarcastically. "Let us state the case, if you please. You are in love with a girl, you say. But you do not go to her frankly and say: 'I love you, but we cannot be married for perhaps a long time. Will you wait for me?' No; you do not even give the girl a hint that you love her. By some mysterious process the young woman is to understand that she is something more dear to you than the dust on the earth. She is to be content to await her lord's pleasure—to fold her hands demurely and simper: 'Some day perhaps he will ask me; let us hope so."

"It does seem unreasonable," admitted the miserable Pennington; "but I should think she would know in some way."

"Not at all; women are not mind-readers. No; your plan is not a good one. As one in love you are not a success. And you are to remember that nice plums are not so very common, and so many like nice plums." She turned her back to him and pretended to adjust the curtain. "It would be wiser to pluck them," she added timidly, "while it is possible, if, indeed, it is possible. And you do not know until you *try*."

Dorothy had no sooner said the words than she could have bitten out her tongue for saying them. It seemed as if she were taking it too much for granted that he was having reference to herself. And if he thought that, he would believe that she were deliberately flinging herself at his head.

Pennington heaved a prodigious sigh and shook his head. “There are reasons why I could not possibly ask her now, final reasons.” He did not even look at her.

She put her hand to her heart as if in pain. He had no reference to herself, then. Otherwise he would certainly have spoken out at that time. She had actually been encouraging him. She had spoken in a manner more than unreserved, in a fashion almost unmaidenly. She walked to the window blushing painfully. Then recovering her self-possession, she turned to him unconcerned and smiling.

“But it is quite a compliment to me, Mr. Senator, that you make me a confidant in your love affairs. One would imagine I were very old, I declare. But let us go back to your friend, Mr. Pennington, the playwright. That is more interesting. Now if you can possibly overcome his diffidence, you will promise me that you will bring him to see me before you leave, won’t you? To take your place, you know. And I do hope that he wont bore me with any love affairs. As one in love, you are not a success, I fear.”

Pennington rose to go. “I know I must appear very ridiculous to you,” he said, ruefully, tugging on his glove. Then trying to speak light-heartedly: “As for Pennington, I will bring him around if I can persuade him to come. He is not much of a chap with the girls, I am afraid—not even with the girl he loves.”

“Oh, but he would care for *me*,” said Dorothy, smiling confidently. “I would *make* him care.”

“You could make my walking-stick care if you wanted to. But I am not sure that I shall be able to bring Pen. around, though I will if possible.”

“Then this may as well be good-bye as good-day, don’t you think so?” she asked flippantly, as they clasp ed hands.

“Perhaps we may as well say good-bye as a precautionary measure,” he said flippantly in his turn, “I have so many things to see to before I go. Good-bye then.”

“Yes, of course. You must have many calls to make; you are so popular. And if I were you, I -would speak frankly to the young lady.”

Pennington shook his head.

“You are very obstinate. Well good-bye. I am so glad to have known you. You have amused me *always*.”

But when the front door slammed, she went upstairs to her room, and flinging herself on the bed, buried her head in her arms.

CHAPTER XVI.

ALL THE WORLD'S A STAGE.

"WELL, I read over that manuscript of yours last night, after the *Courier* went to press," said Richardson.

"What do you think of it?"

Pennington put the question shamefacedly, as if he were hoping against his better judgment.

Richardson lit his pipe which had gone out.

"Well now," he began, with the ominous hesitation, not of one who is weighing his words judicially, but casting about in his mind for something pleasant to say, and finds it difficult. "Well now, the play has its merits. I don't deny that. The treatment of the plot is excellent. You have a style; an eye for situations, but—" He paused.

"The interest flags?" suggested Pennington anxiously.

"No, not exactly that. But you see—" He paused again, puffing vigorously at his pipe.

"Then what is the matter?"

"Why it's this way, old chap. I don't want to say anything to hurt you, but you see it's this way. In the first place I doubt very much if people care about sitting two or three hours listening to a play that, with each succeeding act, plunges them into a deeper fit of the blues. People may like to read about disagreeable things in the newspapers, but they read stories or go to see plays to enjoy themselves, as a rule, to get outside the worries of life, to escape, the disagreeable things."

"That may be all very true. But I had to present life as it looked to me," said Pennington doggedly. "I couldn't write myself down to the level of a Fourteenth Street shopping crowd, could I?"

"Oh come now, old fellow, the Fourteenth Street shopping crowd, as you contemptuously call it, makes up the greater part of the world, doesn't it? The truth of the matter is, Pen., you have been in a beastly morbid mood these past two months, since you came back from abroad, and this morbid mood permeates the whole of 'The Last of One Man's Ambition.'"

"I don't see how I could help it," said Pennington crossly.

"Very likely not. Only you mustn't attempt to succeed with a play in which every character has the potentialities of a deep-dyed villain. There must be the virtuous heroine and the chivalrous hero as well, you know."

"I suppose so," assented Pennington, beginning to smile.

"Besides, don't you see, old fellow," cried Richardson, encouraged by the smile, "you have written of everything about which you know nothing? You have laid your scene back in the seventeenth century. Now honestly, Pen., what do you know about the old colonial[18] days?"

"Precious little, that's a fact."

"Of course you don't. A play like the 'Last of One Man's Ambition,' (ugh, the very title makes me feel gruesome), should take three years' preparation and steady reading. Besides, generally speaking, people want something nearer home—something of human interest that touches every-day life. If you can get a good fresh idea, if you can make your situations dramatic, if you can develop[19] your idea in accordance with the rules of the stage, and especially if you can make people laugh a bit—you have a play that may succeed. But you must have a good fresh idea and human interest."

Pennington picked up the huge roll of manuscript and flung it deliberately in the fire. "You are right, Richardson, and I am an ass," he said cheerfully.

Richardson attempted a feeble rescue of the blazing pages, but his friend pushed him back in his seat.

"Let the thing burn up with all my bad humors and disappointments," he said quietly.

In silence they watched the pages blacken and whirl up the chimney.

"Since the thing is done for," said Richardson at last, "I can't help letting you know that I think it was not worthy of you."

And Pennington himself felt as if a great load were lifted from his shoulders now that the play was out of existence, and as if the world were once more a rather nice place to live in. "Every fellow must fail once, I suppose," he said bravely.

"Now you are beginning to talk like old Pennington again. Fail *once.* That means try once more. Good. You are sure to succeed if you can only get out of the blues."

"You honestly think I have it in me?"

"I haven't a doubt of it, if only you can forget that you made a duffer of yourself over there in Paris, and if you could get over being a love-sick swain."

"You are pretty hard on a fellow. But I am going to try again. And I have just eight and a half months left in which to write a new play. That is, it is that time before I must report to the old gentleman how I have spent his three thousand dollars. And I am determined to have a play to show to him."

"And you will. But there must be no sentimental pessimism this time, no colonial days, mind."

"Supposing that we try to scare up an idea this very night," cried Pennington, growing excited and walking about the room.

"All right. Now let us take the facts of the case as they stand. First of all, we may as well make up our minds that what interests us, will interest other people. That's an axiom. Then we have to ask, what do you know, what have you seen of the world?"

"Well, I have been at college; I have been a reporter more than two years; and I know New York like a book. Then what have I seen of the world? Mighty little except New York. Why, of course, for a couple of months I was abroad spending—"

Pennington stopped short and looked at Richardson. Richardson dropped his pipe and looked at Pennington.

Simultaneously each shouted at the other: "A Cheque for Three Thousand."

In his joy, Pennington picked up Richardson bodily and marched up and down the room with him. Then Richardson in his struggles for liberty, broke the gas-globe and kicked a hole in his hat that had fallen on the floor. Pennington thought he had never seen anything so exquisitely funny, and almost strangled himself on the spot in a convulsive fit of laughter and coughing.

In the midst of this stampede, the janitor appeared with a nice large club.

"An begob, I thought shure t'was somewan a-burglin' and a-murtherin," he said, looking at the two doubtfully.

Pennington was seated on the floor amidst the ruins, coughing and laughing and stamping and crying. Richardson, likewise on the floor, was thumping his friend vigorously on the back.

"It's all right, Mr. Janitor," Richardson said reassuringly between the thumps. "Mr. Pennington has become mildly insane. That is all. He will come around presently. I wouldn't worry, if I were you."

"An' yez don't think as yez need an ambulonce, sor?"

"I think not, thank you. These attacks don't last long. as a rule."

The janitor reluctantly shut the door behind him, and listened behind the key-hole apprehensively.

"And to think that while I have been rummaging the seventeenth century inside out, searching for my ideas, this cheque for three thousand was in my pocket all the time. I shall die of laughing."

"And while you are spending it you are literally writing your play. I never heard of such an idyllic, jolly way of earning money."

"Come now, let's get the situations down on paper at once," cried Pennington. "Title: 'A Cheque for Three Thousand'— that is a foregone conclusion, eh?"

"Well, rather, my boy. Scene I. Eccentric millionaire and philanthropist with money to burn, tired of systematic, sensible money-giving to hospitals and buildings of brick and mortar, plans a more novel and exciting way of getting rid of his superfluous cash."

"And therefore, Wanted: A young man with an ingenuous face and crazy ideas, who looks as if he might spend the money picturesquely."

"Scene II. The restaurant: The young man found. Deigns to accept the great responsibility."

"And Mrs. Harris and Senator Diggle, they will be the low comedy characters, eh?"

"And Dorothy Whitehurst—you should make something fine of her."

"I will. I will draw her to the life. I can make her no finer."

"Only you must change all the names, you know."

"Of course."

And so for an hour, Pennington and Richardson shouted the scenes at each other, every minute becoming more excited.

And when the plot was rudely outlined—and for that matter, never was seen so accommodating a plot; it developed itself—Pennington took out of his drawer a great pile of foolscap, put on his smoking-jacket, pushed Richardson out of the room, and began to plan the acts of "A Cheque for Three Thousand."

Half an hour later, Richardson put his head in at the door, and shouted: "Now Miss Whitehurst mustn't refuse you. This play has to end well, everybody must live happy ever after. We must help out fortune a little."

"All right, old man." Pennington grinned and scribbled away for dear life. "I'll make her accept me. Of stage-land I am the king. All my subjects shall obey me, even Dorothy Whitehurst."

"Now you have the idea," cried Richardson, disappearing with a chuckle.

Another five minutes and he shouted up the stairway: "And I say, it would be the greatest joke in the world to make Dorothy Whitehurst the daughter of the Great Unknown who gave you the money."

"And Mrs. Sally Harris, the second donor, his sister-in-law, eh?"

"Ha, ha, ha!" roared Richardson back. "And you can make Dorothy Whitehurst be at the play the first night, and she can accept you right on the scene of your triumph."

Pennington sprang down the stairs, reckless of the fact that necks sometimes break. "Great idea! I'll do it! Only I can't work to-night. I'm too happy! I feel as if Dorothy had accepted me in real earnest. Dear old fellow, I believe I have struck oil at last. Hurry up and put on your coat, and we'll go to the Clifton and have a bit to eat and drink. Hooray for the 'Cheque for Three Thousand!'"

"So say we all of us: Hooray for the 'Cheque for Three Thousand!'"

And that's how the Great Play came to be written.

CHAPTER XVII.

MANY HAPPY RETURNS OF THE DAY.

On Monday, February 3, 1896, the sun had scarcely squinted over the chimney tops, before Pennington awoke with a start. For several minutes he lay there on his back, blinking sleepily up at the ceiling and wondering what it was that gave him a vague feeling as if something extraordinary was going to happen.

Then it flashed across his mind what it was, and he sat up in his bed smiling broadly, as if the something were very pleasant indeed. And I am sure that if all those people who, at that moment, had reserved seats for a "Cheque for Three Thousand" reposing in their pocket-books under their pillows—if they could have seen that smile—so fresh and jolly and withal so confident—they would have made up their minds then and there not to go away from the play disappointed or indifferent.

There was something else to happen this day to which Pennington had been looking forward somewhat uneasily, it must be confessed. It was just a year ago to-day, that an eccentric gentleman had given him the cheque, and to-day Pennington, according to the promise, was to give an account of himself and to tell how he had spent the money. He felt curiously like the unfaithful steward that we all know about, though during the greater part of the time he had been working manfully to redeem the folly of his two months abroad. And he could not help hoping that his story and adventures might satisfy even the Great Unknown, who, no doubt, was expecting something quite out of the usual to come of his strange experiment in philanthropy.

Pennington was so extremely nervous when dressing, that he quite forgot how to tie his De Joinville, and after he had essayed a bow with no better success, he had to wake up Richardson, who was snoring placidly in the next room, to show him how.

As for shaving himself, that was quite out of the question. Even when he came out of the barber's chair, his face was so hacked up, that if one had been in Germany instead of in New York, one might readily have imagined that he had distinguished himself in a student's duel.

But perhaps we shall not think the less of him if he wriggled and twisted under the razor. Because every time the barber pulled his face this way or that, his eyes could not help meeting huge placards that announced that the farce-comedy, "A Cheque for Three Thousand," written by Norman Bridgworth Pennington, was to be put on the boards for the first time that very night at the Lyric Theatre.

Precisely at nine-thirty in the morning, Pennington drew on a new pair of gloves and started down Broadway for the law office of Howe and Williamson, the meeting place that had been appointed one year before.

He tried not to be conceited nor to look too often at his name, printed in large capitals on the blue placards, but when a funny picture of Mrs. Sally Harris and himself on board the *S. S. New York* confronted him unexpectedly, or Senator Diggle beseeching him to accept the twenty-five thousand dollars to pay the expenses for upholding Napoleonic ideals, it all seemed so real that he could not help smiling and nodding a pleasant "How d'ye do?"

And it was a novel and delicious sensation to run up against dramatic critics and actors and playwrights, who wrung his hand with a warm-hearted, brotherly enthusiasm, and who declared that, judging from the dress rehearsal that they had seen the evening before, they were willing to bet absolutely fabulous and impossible sums that the play had a clear-run ahead it of one hundred-and-fifty nights.

So that when Pennington sat in the private office of Mr. Howe, awaiting the arrival of the Great Unknown, he felt rather important, I am afraid, and talked somewhat patronizingly to the senior partner.

His importance, however, shrunk to pitiably dwarfish proportions, when a messenger-boy returned with a note which stated that the gentleman who had so mysteriously befriended him could not possibly bother with him just then, but would meet him that evening at the same place, unless some other place were designated.

At first Pennington was hurt and savage.

He would have liked to answer that it would be very inconvenient indeed for him to see anyone that evening—that he was to be engaged at the Lyric Theatre instead—that he had fulfilled his part of the contract, and that he had no intention whatever of concerning himself further with the matter. But he did not write anything so impertinent or ungrateful.

He wrote in reply a polite little note, expressing his regret that it was necessary to postpone even for a few hours an interview that he had been looking forward to with so much pleasure. He begged that his unknown benefactor would do him the honor of accepting a box for himself and friends at the Lyric Theatre for that evening. The request must seem strange. But the play to be presented there was written by the writer, and was a tolerably accurate, though, of course, exaggerated account of the adventures the writer had met with in spending the three thousand dollars.

To this modest invitation, Pennington received (after half an hour's impatient waiting) a not too gracious acceptance.

He left the office with a queer misgiving as to the result of the protracted meeting. In some inconceivable way the interview seemed to loom up before his excited imagination as mysteriously portentious—a crisis somehow was involved in it—the crisis of all his future life and happiness.

CHAPTER XVIII.

FACT AND FICTION.

Towards evening, about the time when Richardson was vainly trying to convince Pennington that February the third is *not* the longest day of the year, Mr. Silas Whitehurst alighted cumberously from his coupé; and, fitting his latch-key in the key-hole, threw open his front door and shouted, "Dorothy."

That young lady came tripping downstairs: "What do you want, cross-patch?" she asked, taking his hat and coat.

"Do you suppose that you and your Aunt Sally Harris—there's no use my mentioning your mother, I suppose—are rested enough from your voyage to go to the theatre to-night, child?"

Dorothy linked her arm in the arm of her father and walked upstairs with him to the library. "Well, you know, daddy, we only landed yesterday, and I expect that Aunt Sally does feel rather limp, but what is the play? Something very good?"

"Oh, a silly enough thing, I expect. It is called "A Cheque for Three Thousand." But it happens to have some interest for me. Mr. Whitehurst threw himself in an arm-chair and bit off the end of a cigar.

"Why?" asked Dorothy, holding a lighted match for him.

Mr. Whitehurst enveloped himself in a cloud of smoke to hide his embarrassment. "Now you mustn't tell your mother, child," he whispered hoarsely, "but it is this way. One year ago in a restaurant in Bleecker Street, I gave a young fellow whom I had never set eyes on before, a cheque for three thousand dollars. And what's more, I told him he could do what he wanted with it."

Dorothy held up her hands. "You wicked, extravagant man! And you pretended that you couldn't afford the money for my bracelet."

"But you got the bracelet all right enough, child, so don't grumble."

"And what has he done with the money?"

"I don't know yet. He had to promise that one year from the day I gave him the money he would come and tell me. To-day the year is up.

"You romantic old dear, and didn't the ungrateful thing come and tell you?" asked Dorothy anxiously, seating herself on the arm of his chair.

"He was to see me this morning at the office of my attorneys. But I had to put off the meeting because of business."

"Oh, what a pity! So you will *never* know what he did with the money. How disappointing."

"Wait a bit, child. Don't be illogical. I asked if he couldn't give me another meeting, and he has written me that he will see me at the Lyric Theatre to-night."

"How funny! I never heard of *anything* so funny. I never supposed that men ever chose the theatre as a place to tell each other things.

"There you go again. I wonder if a woman *could* be logical, if she wanted to. There was method in the fellow's madness. I forgot to say that I gave him that money so that he could have a chance to write a play. It seems the fellow has written his play—which is more than I expected when I gave him the money—and he says that the incidents of this play give a pretty fair idea of how the money was spent."

"But I don't understand *at all*, I—"

"There you are again. Illogical as ever. I don't believe a woman could follow an argument if she wanted to. But here's his letter. See. if; that explains things and don't bother me any more."

Dorothy dropped the letter with a little scream.

"Norman B. Pennington! Why that's Senator Diggle's best friend. So he *did* write the play after all and he has made something nice of himself. I'm so awfully glad. I can't tell why. And here are tickets for a box. Of course we'll go. I never heard of anything so perfectly thrilling. And you gave him the money, you dear, kind, old philanthropist."

"Go away and leave me alone, child. I want to read my newspaper. Do you know this Pennington fellow?"

"No; I don't. Senator Diggle wouldn't introduce him for some reason. But I wanted to meet him very much. And he is Senator Diggle's friend. Shall we meet him, do you think? He will be sure to know where *he* is."

"Do you want to drive me crazy, child? Why can't you explain yourself? Now who is he?"

"He—why that is—that is," Dorothy hesitated and rumpled up her father's gray hair.

"Oh, the millionaire who was sweet on you, and who jilted you to go to Africa to shoot lions."

"Yes," said Dorothy in a low voice. "Only you mustn't say he was sweet on me. That's horrid; besides, it isn't true."

"Well, well, we all have our little disappointments. But my Dorothy jilted. Ha, ha."

"I *wasn't* jilted and I am *not* disappointed," cried Dorothy indignantly, "and it isn't kind of you to say so." She ran out of the room.

"I wonder if the silly child cares for the fellow yet," said Mr. Whitehurst, settling down to his papers.

CHAPTER XIX.

BUT TRUTH IS NICER THAN FICTION.

Behind the scenes of the Lyric Theater was the excitement that usually characterizes a "first night."

At fifteen minutes past eight, the orchestra began the overture. "Now, then," demanded the manager, cautiously looking around, "is everything ready? Then ring her up." And the curtain rolled up on the first act of "A Cheque for Three Thousand."

But ten minutes before this supreme moment, Pennington had left the theatre. The manager had found him crouched behind a piece of scenery and shivering like a baby before its morning bath. The manager looked him over critically.

"I've seen 'em like this many a time before, Mr. Pennington. And although if my experience goes for anything, you and I are going to put a nice little pile of bills in our pockets as a result of this evening, the best thing you can do is to get out of it. Go down to the café, or take a walk for an hour. You will find *that* hard enough. But it isn't so hard on your nerves as waiting here."

Pennington slunk out of the stage-door into, the street like any criminal. There the cars were clanging and cabs were rushing to and fro. People were laughing and talking just as unconcernedly as if the "Cheque for Three Thousand" were a paltry piece of commercial paper for that amount lying smugly in the vaults of the bank opposite.

"I will walk around the block twenty times," declared Pennington grimly. "That must take an hour."

Three times he had stalked the distance, brushing aside women and thumping deliberately into men. He was half around the fourth time —directly behind the great theater—when, was that laughter? Applause? Or was it derision? He dared not listen—the suspense was terrible.

He looked about him frantically.

"Keb, sir?" said a night-hawk, glancing over the box of his hansom.

"Yes, yes! Drive me anywhere. Drive me to Jerusalem. Drive me to Harlem. Drive me anywhere. Only drive like Jehu, and I'll give you twice your fare."

The cabman had never heard of Jehu, but he turned into Twenty-seventh Street and whipped his horse up the avenue, reckless of the shouts of the policeman that followed him. He had reached the Plaza, when Pennington yelled to him to return. Down the avenue the cab tore again, sparks flying from the horses' hoofs, cabby's whip crackling, Pennington's heart quaking. But only to be arrested at the theater door for breaking the ordinances.

Five, blessed, mortal minutes Pennington shouted at the policeman and the policeman shouted back at him.

In the midst of the wrangle, Richardson dashed up frantic. He grasped the situation at a glance.

"They're calling for you, Pen.," he cried, tears of excitement streaming down his cheeks. And pushing the indignant officer of the law against the lobby, he dragged the bewildered Pennington through the stage-door, and hustled him, limp and brainless, behind the scenes.

There the manager was laughing and gesticulating and swearing and shaking hands with everybody; and the stage-manager in his shirt sleeves was calling silence and making twice as much noise as all the rest put together. And all the while cries of "Author, author," came in a muffled roar through the great curtain.

"Here he is," grasped the breathless Richardson, pushing his friend forward.

"Has it failed?" whispered Pennington, pale to the roots of his hair.

"Failed! Failed," shouted the manager.

"Listen to that racket, will you? Do people yell like that when a thing has *failed?* Come, come now, Mr. Pennington, try to brace up, sir. You've got to make your little bow, you know. Pull aside the curtain, some one. There you are, Mr. Pennington, just a word to cheer 'em up for waiting so long."

He shoved Pennington on the stage through the opening made for him.

Limp and pale, with his teeth chattering with fright, Pennington stood before his enthusiastic applauders, a sorry figure. He made a desperate effort to pull himself together, smiling like a doll of sawdust, and bobbing his head up and down in what he vainly imagined to be a bow.

The people demanded a speech.

Pennington thrust his hands in his pockets; pulled them out; twirled his thumbs; put his hands in his pockets again; moved his lips; and—was silent.

"Haul him back, some one," whispered the manager. "The boy's crazy. His success has turned his head."

Indeed Pennington's conduct seemed to justify the contempt.

He ran to the curtain that had been let down, screwed his right eye at the hole that looked out on the audience; gazed around on the wondering stage-hands as if he were dreaming; screwed his left eye at the hole again, and rushed from the stage.

"Stark crazy, poor chap," said the manager, shaking his head.

Pennington threw open the door that led to the foyer—ran madly toward a box; retreated; hid behind a pillar; wrung his hands in ecstasy; ran out again; hugged himself; took a deep breath; and then literally sprang, jumped, tumbled into a box.

"Miss Whitehurst, Dorothy!" he gasped.

"Mr. Senator!" she cried.

"Diggle, my dear!" screamed Mrs. Harris.

"*Mr.* Pennington!" thundered Silas Whitehurst.

"Sir!" faltered Pennington.

Mrs. Sally Harris fell on his neck. She wept copiously. She laughed hysterically. She kissed him on both cheeks. "An' I *can* keep a secret, and don't you go denying it, Diggle, my dear. Six mortal hours have I been dyin' to tell Dorothy, and it ain't easy on your nerves."

Dorothy turned pale and then a fiery red, thought she was going to faint, made up her mind that she would not, frowned, laughed, held out her hand, tried to speak—and then sat down ignominiously, trembling.

Mr. Silas Whitehurst grasped his cane firmly, thumped the floor, grasped Pennington by the collar, shook him, shook his cane, half choked himself in his excitement, half choked Pennington, then roared hoarsely: "You young rascal, how dared you?"

"Eh?" sputtered Pennington.

"So *this* is your gratitude, is it? I give you three thousand dollars and in return you make fun of me—to my face. You young rascal."

"You—*you* give me a cheque? Do you mean to say that you are the Great Unknown? *You?*"

"Come, come, you miscreant, you—you Janus-faced young miscreant, don't pretend that you didn't know it."

Pennington wondered if softening of the brain was imminent. He couldn't think. "Do you mean to say?" he began.

"You *know* it. It was in the play. But who told you is beyond me."

"Do you mean to say that *you* are Dorothy's—I mean Miss Whitehurst's father, and that you gave me that cheque? Dorothy Whitehurst's *father* gave me that cheque."

"Don't be a hypocrite, young man. It was in the play. You know it."

"Then upon my word and honor, sir, this is simply the last of this most extraordinary series of coincidences. I had no idea—not the remotest idea of the truth of it when I wrote the play. It a was suggested to me by a friend, to give the play a climax, to make it a little more dramatic. Truth is stranger than fiction this evening, it seems. Dorothy— Whitehurst's—father —gave—me—that—cheque."

"And to think, Diggle, that 'twas Si's dead cousin's wife that gave you t'other two thousand pounds," cried Mrs. Harris.

"So that was true, also, was it?" demanded Mr. Whitehurst, grimly.

Pennington stared.

"You young rogue. Then not content with getting three thousand out of me, you wheedle twice as much out of poor old Sally. And do you know, young man, that I thought my daughter had a millionaire in tow. And all the time it was my scapegoat." Here, Mr. Whitehurst's indignation threatened to put an end to his career.

Dorothy grasped her father's arm. "If you please, papa," she cried, entreatingly.

Pennington grasped the other arm. "Oblige me by saying no more. The play shall be withdrawn at once. I can at least make that reparation. Though when I tell you that I never dreamed of putting you to any annoyance—*you*, of all people." Pennington looked steadily at Dorothy.

Dorothy cast down her eyes and then looked at him bravely. "Indeed, Mr. Senator, I mean Mr. Pennington, we shall never dream of allowing you to withdraw your play. No one could imagine for a moment that the characters are really ourselves. And I am sure that papa is proud in his heart of hearts that you have—*have* made something nice of yourself, after all."

"Besides what's the hodds so long as we're all 'appy? It's all in the fambly, my dear," cried Mrs. Harris, beaming on Pennington.

"Then I will alter such parts as Mr. Whitehurst finds objectionable," said Pennington, gratefully.

"What! Alter my play?" Mr. Whitehurst thumped his cane on the floor emphatically. "You shan't change a word. It's gospel truth as it stands. How dare you suggest such a thing? *My* play! All out of my three thousand! Ha, ha, ha!"

"But only a minute ago, you were so mad that you tried to choke me to death," cried Pennington, rather bewildered at the turn affairs were taking.

"You are a blockhead, sir. I wasn't doing any such thing. Can't a man be excited if he wants to? Tell me that. What will Smith say when he hears of the fruits of the three thousand? I'll bring him to see my play. All out of my three thousand. You young rascal. My play!"

"Then I need make no changes?" asked Pennington, looking anxiously at Dorothy.

"You shan't change me, Diggle, you mind that," threatened Mrs. Harris. "There ain't a person in the play more amoosing than me. You shan't change me, or I'll change my will."

"Of course he shan't change it. I want Smith to see it as it stands. My play! Well, well, if they are not turning out the lights. Now, then, Sally, are you going to tattle all night? It takes the women-folks to talk. Come home with us and take supper, and tell me some more about that ass Diggle. My play! Ha, ha!"

Mrs. Sally Harris followed the cousin of her late husband, declaring that she was only a lonely old woman, and that if she chose to take a fancy to a young fellow who was the very image of the defunct Bob, why she had more money than was good for her, and that even if the name Pennington was not akin to Harris, it was all in the family.

But Pennington whispered to Dorothy: "Do you think that the play wants changing very much, Miss Whitehurst, dear Miss Whitehurst?"

"I—I don't think that *very* much alteration is needed," faltered Dorothy.

"I've grown a little since I saw you last. I can reach up to some plums now. But the sweetest of them all dangles far out of reach still, I fear. Or ought I to try and reach it? One cannot tell if it is possible till one tries. Miss Whitehurst, dear Miss Whitehurst, Dorothy, dearest, sweetest Dorothy, do you still like intrepid men?"

"Y—Yes," whispered Dorothy, blushing in the dark.

"Then tell me, my own, own Dorothy, do you think that the play need be altered at all?

Do you like the ending?" Pennington felt for her hand.

"Yes," answered Dorothy, squeezing his fingers, "and oh, Norman, I'm so glad that your name isn't *really* Diggle."

THE END.

Transcriber's Notes.

Most of the author's original material remains intact, along with many antiquated spellings. The following items however, have been intentionally changed, or corrected, for the sake of readability. Punctuation has also been changed.

[1] Page 6: Changed "businesss" to "business"
[2] Page 16: Updated "gayety" to "gaiety"
[3] Page 18, 33: Changed "ecstacy" to "ecstasy"
[4] Page 18: Changed "millioniare" to "millionaire"
[5] Page 20: Changed "is'nt" to "isn't"
[6] Page 21: Changed "had became" to "had become"
[7] Page 24: Changed "mausolem" to "mausoleum"
[8] Page 29: Changed "panetella" to "panatella"
[9] Page 30: Changed "monieur's" to "monsieur's"
[10] Page 32: Changed "desparingly" to "despairingly"
[11] Page 33: Changed "colums" to "column"
[12] Page 34: Updated "stateman" to "statesman"
[13] Page 37: Changed "goddesss" to "goddess"
[14] Page 39: Changed "Bridgeworth" to "Bridgworth"
[15] Page 43: Changed "would'nt" to "wouldn't"
[16] Page 44: Changed "does'nt" to "doesn't"
[17] Page 44: Changed "had'nt" to "hadn't"
[18] Page 59: Changed "colonnial" to "colonial"
[19] Page 60: Changed "develope" to "develop"

"A Cheque for Three Thousand."
by Arthur Henry Veysey.
Published in 1899
by G. W Dillingham, New York.

Transcribed and edited by
Jeffrey Merrow, November 2014.

Tadalique and Company, Publishers.
http://tadalique.com/

Questions? Feedback?
Contact:
webmaster@tadalique.com